WE'LL BEGIN AGAIN

LAURÈN LEE

Thank you!
Margaret!

[signature]

ISBN-10: 1985572974

ISBN-13: 978-1985572973

❀ Created with Vellum

For all the American Veterans—
You are not forgotten

PROLOGUE

Snowflakes floated delicately downward from the sky and twin-kled under the tall street lamps, which glittered in the man's deso-late eyes. His father always told him as a child that each snowflake was unique, and no two were ever the same. The minutes wore on, and each frigid flake clung together and stuck to the ground, coating the sidewalk in feathery dust.

The man shivered and pulled the ratty blanket tighter around his body. The cold shook his being to the bones, and he wondered if he'd ever be warm again.

The bench he laid on held his frail body with ease. During the day, mothers and children, business professionals and wanderers claimed the benches as their own, But, at night, it was his. This bench was his couch, his bed, his castle, his home.

The man blinked rapidly as the flakes clung to his eyelashes. The heavenly precipitation reflected in his eyes, as did the waning moon glowing in the sky. His beard caught flakes, too. It grew well past his chin; he didn't have access to a razor. His frozen dog tags lay against his neck. At one time, he would have given anything to trade the desert for the snow. Now, he wished for the sun and the sand.

Laughter echoed in the distance. He imagined a group of friends pouring out of the pub, hand in hand and arms laced through each other's. They probably had a few drinks together after work. Maybe they had families to go home to and maybe not. They were thick as thieves, and they all had a warm bed calling their names.

He forgot how alcohol tickled his tongue during the first sip. Hell, he couldn't remember the last warm meal he consumed. Every morning, he hunted for breakfast behind cafes and in their dumpsters for fresh scraps. Lunch and dinner were harder to come by. He'd been shooed away more times than he could count. No one wanted him loitering around their restaurants. Bad for business.

He closed his eyes and settled in for another brutal night, alone on the streets and under the starry night's sky. While the weather chilled, the idea of another lonely night made him feel even more broken.

Chapter One

WILLIAM

September eleventh changed my life. And not in the way the average American felt the day a group of sick fuck terrorists crashed into the towers. My pain was different; my father was in the first tower that fell. But, wait, it gets worse: September eleventh is also my birthday.

At eighteen years old, I had no goals, no dreams, no desires. I was a kid about to become a man and had no idea what I wanted out of life. Most of my friends planned on going to law school or becoming a doctor. Me? I just wanted to play video games and drink Monster until I crashed.

My indecisiveness infuriated my parents. My mom, an executive assistant, and my dad, a businessman, wanted me to grow up to be successful enough to move out and buy a house of my own. My father, in particular, had an incredible work ethic. While his hard work and dedication to his job positively impacted his company, it didn't always benefit our family. I spent countless nights as a child sitting by my window, waiting to see my father stride up to our front door.

My parents wanted me to be rich, just like them. Money didn't matter to me, though. Maybe because I'd grown up affluent, or perhaps because I didn't feel like I needed it to be happy. I don't know. All I thought back then was my future was far away, so why worry about it?

Even though my parents pressured me about adulthood, my childhood *was incredible. My favorite moments? The simple ones. Like, one day my father came home early from work, which was incredibly rare, and took me out of school. We called my mom at her office and told her there was an emergency, and she had to come home right away. When she arrived, Dad and I had ordered a pizza and picked out a bunch of movies from Block-buster. Naturally, my mom wasn't thrilled about how we enticed her to leave work, but she was so surprised, all she could do was laugh. We blew off our responsibilities for the day and had a movie marathon on the couch.*

Or, another time, a massive snowstorm hit the city and snowed us in for a few days. The power went out soon after the local anchor announced the school closings in our area. At first, I was scared without power, but my mom lit candles all around our brownstone. We played board games under the subtle flames around us and napped together on a nest of fleece blankets I created on the floor. When the power eventually came back on, I cried like a little girl. I wanted to spend more time with my parents in the dark. Without cell phones, without the computer, and yes, without the TV.

The simple days were my favorite days.

In the fall of 2001, I enrolled, with some difficulty, as a freshman at NYU. I had average grades, played sports in high school and joined a club or two my senior year. With the help of my grandparents, my mom's parents, NYU reluctantly accepted me. I'm sure the hefty donation my Papa and Nana sent helped. I hadn't chosen a major yet, so I registered for electives. This didn't please my parents. They constantly urged me to pick a major as though the world would end the very next day. Little did we know, it would.

That Tuesday started off like any other day of the week. It was my birthday, and my only plans consisted of going to my favorite Italian spot around the block with my parents for dinner. I wasn't huge on birthdays. I didn't like the attention. I had a few classes in the morning: Biology and Intro to Psychology. Bio started at eight in the morning. I wanted to skip, but I missed the last two lectures. My professor didn't take attendance, but I realized if I missed too many classes I'd fall too far behind to catch up. Biology bored me to death; I didn't want to torture myself having to teach myself at home.

I lugged my lean, six-foot-three body out of bed, dressed in a pair of dirty jeans and a black V-neck tee shirt. I sniffed under my arms and wrinkled my nose. Unfortunately, I didn't have time to shower, but it was just a dumb class. Wasn't like I went to campus to scout for chicks. Most of the girls at NYU were too stuck up for my taste, anyway.

I loved living so close to campus. The short distance between home and school allowed me to walk on fair weather days and take in the one-of-a-kind city sights along the way. The vendors, the coffee shops, the hustle and bustle of the city took my breath away.

The lecture that Tuesday centered around the endocrine system. I nearly fell asleep on my desk. Professor Binds spoke with one of the most monotonous voices I'd ever heard. If someone wasn't snoring ten minutes into the lecture, then pigs were flying across the Brooklyn Bridge.

Class wrapped up around 8:40; I decided to skip Psych. I wanted to visit my dad at work and surprise him. I hadn't visited his office in quite some time, but I figured he could possibly take an early lunch, and we could hang out. It was my birthday, after all. How could he say no? But, once I walked outside and into the city air, something seemed very wrong. My bones ached with anxiety.

Sirens screeched in the distance; smoke billowed into the brilliant blue sky, and everywhere I looked, people pointed in the direction of the World Trade Center. I held my breath and peered in that direction, too. Then I saw it: the smoke was coming from the towers. Girls cried, and mass panic had begun to spread like wildfire. I stood frozen. The smoke was coming from a part of the building I knew quite well. Without a doubt, I knew the fire and flames licked a floor of the tower I'd visited often. I could point out my father's office in a picture of the World Trade Center in the blink of an eye. In my very core, I knew my father was dead.

Chapter Two

AMELIA

"Charlie, are you almost ready?"

"Yes, Mom!"

"Are you almost ready, or are you 'Charlie ready?'"

"Uh, maybe somewhere in the middle?"

Every morning I struggled to motivate my bright-eyed, blonde-haired fourth grader to climb out of bed, dress, brush his teeth and gather his schoolwork. I sounded like a broken record when I called out and asked for a status. I, on the other hand, had no problem getting ready in the morning. That is, until today.

Our apartment, still lined with packed boxes, created a maze for Charlie and me to weave around. If we walked through without knocking anything to the floor, it was a miracle. We only moved here two weeks ago. Today was Charlie's first day at a new school, and it was my first day at a new job.

Despite moving to a new city, Charlie's routine remained the same, and he still couldn't be ready on time if his life depended on it. Some things never change no matter how much distance is put between your past and future. However, I couldn't afford to be late. What kind of professional was late on their first day of work?

"Charlie, I mean it! We have to leave in T minus five minutes!"

"I heard you the first couple of times!" Charlie shot back.

"Did you? Because you're still not out here tying your shoes yet, mister!"

I tossed and turned for hours and hours last night. I couldn't help but wonder what my new boss would be like or how my coworkers would treat me. I thought about what kind of coffee the office provided. Did they have K-cups or coffee grounds? As if that's an important life decision to make.

A whirlwind by the name of Charlie flew around the corner and into my arms.

"Ready!"

"You're getting heavy, kiddo."

"That's because I eat my vegetables and drink milk."

"You do?" I gazed at him suspiciously.

"Well, sometimes I do."

I set him down and ruffled his soft, blond hair. When I found out I was pregnant, all I cared about was having a healthy child. I didn't care if it was a boy or a girl or if they looked like me or not. Charlie was the best damn thing to come from my failed marriage. Silver lining.

"You look pretty, Mama."

"Thanks, Tater Tot."

I spun around dramatically as my navy pencil skirt hugged my hips. My dirty-blonde hair twirled, and my leather heels clacked against the floor while I made a full turn. Looking in the mirror this morning, I realized the woman I wanted to be returned my gaze. I'd curled my elbow-length hair, put on makeup and spritzed my favorite Chanel perfume on the nape of my neck. While I'd developed a few wrinkles since my prime, I continued to smile brightly despite my age. I never thought I'd miss dressing up, but after weeks of moving and wearing nothing but sweatpants, my feminine side purred.

Growing up, my mother reminded me of my beauty, but never forgot to reiterate the importance of being healthy, too. When I found the time, I worked out at the gym or ran outside. Before Charlie, I almost had a six pack, which I proudly revealed at the beach or by the pool. Now, the six pack is more of a two-pack, but I've done what I could. After all, there were only so many hours in the day, and between raising a child on my own and working my ass off, there wasn't always time for myself.

"Ready for your first day?"

"I hope I make new friends," Charlie whimpered.

"You will, babe. Just like you made new friends at your last school, you'll make new ones here, too."

When a recruiter called me and said a law firm several hundred miles away had an opening for a corporate attorney, I told them I wasn't interested. How could I move my child across the country in the middle of the school year? I had excellent credentials, though, and a phenomenal win/loss ratio. The recruiter called me every day, upping the ante with better benefits, higher pay, and other opportunities I'd be afforded if I accepted their offer.

"Isn't there someone more qualified? Surely I can't be the only attorney who'd fit the bill?"

"Ms. Montgomery, the partners want you and only you. You stirred the pot after that case last month, and my bosses want you on their staff."

Hint: I helped one of the largest technology companies in the country acquire another smaller business and their accompanying patents. The buyout cost more than four hundred and fifty million dollars. And yes, I got it done in record time.

After weeks of coaxing and a phone interview with the managing partner, I finally said yes. Once I realized I'd have the chance to start fresh somewhere far away from my ex, I accepted the job with no regrets. It took another few weeks for Charlie's dad to agree. I think he fought me for the sake of argument; he only hosted Charlie two weekends a month as it was. Not to mention, he planned to remarry in a little over two months, so he was tied up with planning. Good thing he had one marriage under his belt so he'd know what to do the second time around. Cue the bitterness I still carried with me. We divorced less than two years ago, and now he was engaged to remarry? The man worked fast, not that I could blame him.

Anyway, Charlie, my partner in crime, and I were leaving on a jet plane and headed to the big city.

Chapter Three

AMELIA

Charlie jumped into the backseat with his iPad in tow. He never left home without the damn thing. Sometimes, I wish I never bought him one. Weren't kids supposed to play outside, roll in the dirt and make a mess? My kid's eyes were glued to it. More often than not, I pried it out of his tiny fingers, which naturally sent him into a fit of rage.

"How's your game?" I questioned dryly.

"Can't talk. I'm on level twenty-eight, and I'm about to face the boss."

"Alrighty then," I trailed off and turned the radio on a little louder. Even though my son didn't want to talk to me, I'd grasp entertainment in the form of singing my heart out to the newest pop song that I didn't remotely know the words to. Charlie giggled in the back seat while his thumbs pounded furiously on his game console.

Charlie's new school was located a few blocks away from our new apartment. With a new city, though, comes new traffic patterns. It took twenty minutes to reach the elementary school, which happened to be enough time for the boss to face destruction.

"Okay, kiddo. Hand it over," I said.

"Do I have to?" He pouted.

"Yes. You know the rules. No taking the tablet to school." The last time I let Charlie bring his prized possession to class, he was caught red-handed playing Angry Birds during Math. I believed his punishment was fair and just: I banned him from ever bringing it to school again.

I know, I know. I'm a mean mom.

"Do you want me to walk you in?"

"I'm not a baby, Mom. Sheesh!" Charlie rolled his eyes. Even though he physically took after me, the eye-rolling was purely his father. I had to speak to him about that soon. I couldn't have my son acting like a jerk. More importantly, I didn't want my son acting like his dad.

"I'll be here to pick you up before the after-school program ends, okay?"

I stretched to reach the back seat and kissed Charlie on the cheek.

"Bye, Mom!"

Just like that, my boy started a new school. He didn't even want me to hold his hand.

Damn.

I checked the clock on my dashboard and realized time alluded me. I thought I set aside enough time for taking Charlie to school, but it seemed as though traffic didn't care about my plans. I sped to make it on time. The irony wasn't lost on me: an attorney breaking the law. Hardy-har-har.

I flew downtown in record time and scored the very last spot in the ramp a block away from my new firm. I'd heard I would have trouble finding parking, but that was an understatement. My pulse quickened, and I grabbed my purse, my Vera Bradley lunch tote, my briefcase, and lukewarm coffee.

Please don't be late on your first day, I thought.

It took less than a block for me to realize heels were a bad choice. I limped and moaned with every painful step. When you don't wear stilettos for a while, it's fairly easy to lose your sense of balance. You also forget how much they hurt like an SOB. Tomorrow, I'd wear comfy shoes for the walk to work and bring my pumps to change into once I reached my office. Some days, I'm Super Mom and the Queen of the World. Others? I'm a hot freakin' mess.

The twenty-story building shone brightly from a block away. The sun reflected off the shiny windows, and it stood like a beautiful beacon of hope. My heart thudded with excitement as my fresh start, my new beginning, my sequel stood tall before me.

Out of the corner of my eye, I caught rustling movement upon a park bench under a handful of oak trees. A man, or at least, I thought it was a man, pulled a sleeping bag up toward his neck, covering his body. The burgundy bag caught my attention; my father owned the exact same one.

Growing up, my father tried to teach me how to camp, "try" being the keyword. The outdoors never appealed to me like they did to my dad. He loved hunting season especially. On my twelfth birthday, my dad surprised me by taking me out to the mountains for a daylight hike followed by an overnight camping expedition. He bought me a matching burgundy sleeping bag, and we spent the entire night gazing at the stars and telling stories. After he passed, I couldn't bring myself to throw away the sleeping bag, even though my father's ghost lingered inside its cozy lining. The man on the bench slept inside the same exact one; I could spot that brand from a mile away.

Back home, homeless people were not a rare occurrence, but there was something about this man that struck me; maybe it was the sleeping bag, or maybe it was the long dog tag necklace hanging from his neck. At a glance, I cringed for the man frozen to his bones. I shivered despite wearing a full-length down coat. I could only imagine how *he* felt. Had he been outside all night? How did he lose his home? Wasn't there anyone out in the world who could help him? Take him in? Dozens of questions swirled in my head as I walked past him. Winter had only just begun. This man would suffer many more abysmal nights before the weather broke.

Here I was walking to my new cozy job while another human being woke up underneath a tree. Damn, life was cruel sometimes.

Chapter Four

AMELIA

I walked into the building, with the man outside still on my mind. For the time being, I tried to shake him out of my thoughts. I needed to focus on making an excellent first impression and start my first day with a bang.

"Hi, I'm Amelia Montgomery. Today is my first day." I smiled at the young receptionist wearing Barbie pink lipstick at the front desk.

"Amelia! We are so happy to have you! Let me call up to Ross and let him know you're here."

Wow, she was friendly. If half the staff bore this much cheer, I might have found the best place to work in the world.

I sat in a cozy leather chair beside the fireplace near reception. My first instinct was to bite my fingernails, but I silently scolded myself.

Don't mess up your fresh manicure, dummy.

I sat on my hands to remove the temptation and wondered what my new boss would be like. Sure, I spoke to Ross on the phone, but we never met face-to-face during the interviewing process. He said my resume spoke for itself. At first, I suspected it was all some big ruse to mess up my life. I mean, how many people willingly hire someone without meeting them at least once in person? I guess all my hard work paid off, though. This place seemed incredible, and I hadn't explored past the front desk. I admired the high ceilings and out-of-this-world architecture. It must have been built decades ago but continued to maintain its glamorous prestige.

"Amelia! You're here!"

"Hi, Ross. It's so wonderful to finally meet you," I said shyly and stood to shake his hand.

"Follow me. I'll show you to your office then give you a tour of the building."

For the next hour, Ross walked me all around the premises. He showed me my new office, which provided a spectacular view of the city's skyline. The skyscrapers and architecture painted the horizon and glittered under the sun. He walked me to the on-site cafeteria, bought me another coffee, and introduced me to a handful of new colleagues.

Everyone was super friendly. At my last law firm, I was convinced the Grinch procreated and every one of his children worked there. Here, though, welcoming vibes danced in the air.

After the introductions, Ross walked me back to my office. "I hope you'll be happy here, Amelia."

"I can't imagine not being happy here!"

"Oh! One more thing," Ross said. "Community involvement is very important to us here at the firm. We encourage all of our legal staff to volunteer at a local establishment in the city."

He laid down a couple of brochures on my desk. The top pamphlet caught my eye: a man not so dissimilar to the one with the burgundy sleeping bag adorned the front cover. "Home for the Homeless" was printed across the glossy paper.

"That sounds wonderful," I said. "Where do you volunteer?"

"I spend my Sundays at the nursing home around the corner," Ross said.

"How generous of you! I'll take some time to think about where I'd like to try and let you know as soon as I can."

"Wonderful. Happy to have you here, Amelia. Enjoy the rest of your day."

The morning flew by, and once I finally had the chance to catch my breath, I realized lunchtime had arrived. I thought back to the man I saw outside and wondered what he'd be doing for lunch. Would he eat lunch? Guilt launched itself into my subconscious as I ordered a gourmet chicken and avocado salad from the cafeteria on the first floor of the historic building. My Vera Bradley tote housed some snacks and a bottle of water.

I sat by myself at a cozy corner table away from the hustling and bustling of the cash-out line. I brought my briefcase with me to peruse in while I ate my lunch. For as long as I could remember, all my lunches were work lunches. I didn't have it in me to put my work aside, not even for a half hour to eat.

I closed my eyes and stifled a moan after I took the first bite of my salad. Surely cafeterias weren't supposed to provide such excellent cuisine, right? I could get used to this!

After a few more bites, I slowed my pace and searched around for a specific case file I wanted to examine. Last year, I served as lead attorney on another bombshell case involving the CEO of a well-known environmental company. The CEO, a wealthy, cocky sonofabitch, skimmed off the company's profits despite his already growing six-figure salary. It wasn't often that I veered into criminal law, but the board hired my firm, and specifically me, to sue the CEO and retrieve the stolen funds. I won.

I needed to study my notes, though, because Ross brought up the case this morning during my tour of the office. He mentioned they might have a similar case in the works, and if the firm landed the proposal, he'd make me point person for the legal team.

I needed to refresh my memory and be ready for my meeting with Ross and a few other attorneys tomorrow morning. I assumed we'd be meeting about this potential case. If so, I had no time to waste. Throughout my career, I learned it's always better to be prepared and not need to be, than to be underprepared and embarrass yourself.

I glanced outside to see fluttering snowflakes fall from the sky. I thought about the homeless man again and shivered. Was he still outside? How did he avoid hypothermia being out there for so long? I wondered what I could do to help him. I tapped my nails against the table and furrowed my brows.

The clock struck two in the afternoon, and I realized the cafeteria workers packed up the salad bar and wrapped up the leftover hot entrees. Without hesitation, I jumped up and called out, "Wait!"

The kitchen staff whipped around to see where the spontaneous shouting came from. I waved my arm, and one man with a pristine chef's hat waved and smiled.

"Need something else, ma'am?"

I winced at the greeting but ignored it. "Can I have a turkey sandwich, please?"

"You didn't like the salad?" He appeared crestfallen.

"Oh, no! I loved it. I just, uh, wanted something to bring home for dinner," I lied.

His eyes lit up. "Ah, I see. Not a problem. What would you like on it?"

I never enjoyed ordering for another person. For example, I loved onions, but I know some people who would rather throw away something tainted with them than pick them off. How was I supposed to know what the man on the bench liked or disliked? I had to take the best guess, though.

"Lettuce, tomato, and light onion, please. Oh, and some mayo and oil on the side." I reminded myself to grab plastic silverware before leaving the cafeteria. How rude would it be to give the man condiments without something to use to spread them on the sandwich?

"All set. Enjoy!"

I thanked the chef and climbed the stairs from the cafeteria to the door that led outside. My heart pounded with weariness with every step I took. What would I say to him? Would he accept my offering? What if he was mean and scary? Oh, hell. I sounded like a little girl afraid to ring the doorbell of a neighbor as I tried to hit my quota of Girl Scout cookie sales.

I opened the door to the street and peeked my head outside. I peered to the left and the right as my hands shook. To the right, I saw the bench and craned my neck to see if my friend sat there or not. The bench appeared vacated, and my heart plummeted. Of course, why did I expect him to sit there all day? Undoubtedly, he left and did something with his free time during the day.

Well, now what?

I wasn't going to eat the sandwich, but I also didn't want to throw it away. Then, I saw it: a man across the street digging through the dumpster of a sports bar whose neon sign appeared turned off.

Fuck.

The poor guy had to scavenge for food, of course. What could I do now? I glanced at the man, to his bench and back again. I scurried down the street toward the bench, hoping he wouldn't catch me encroaching on his domain. I reached his spot and found a foul odor hung in the air. I brushed the accumulated snow off the bench with the elbow of my Michael Kors winter coat and left the sandwich on the wooden planks. Hopefully, he'd see it sitting here. And, by the looks of him, I don't think he'd hesitate to have a fresh meal.

In the next moment, my phone vibrated in my pocket. I struggled to pull off my leather gloves and reach for my iPhone, but I grabbed it just in time. The caller ID read, "Reception."

"Hello?" I answered breathlessly.

"Hi, Amelia. Your 2:30 is here to see you."

"Oh, right. I just stepped outside for a few minutes, but I'll be back in my office soon. Send them up in about ten minutes?"

"Sounds good!"

I couldn't stay to find out if the man found my offering. I had to run to my office and prepare to meet with my first client. Hopefully, he'd find it okay and enjoy every last crumb. Fingers crossed.

Chapter Five

WILLIAM

The stench of garbage and spoiled food permeated the air and clung to my shabby clothing. Sometimes, the sports bar across the street from my bench tossed out their leftover chips and salsa from the previous night. It took several attempts at digging through their dumpster to come up empty-handed.

My stomach growled as I ambled across the street with my head down. Some pedestrians stared, but I tried my best to avoid their eyes. As I reached my bench, I noticed a white package on the wooden planks. I gazed around to see if the messenger lingered, but found no one in the vicinity who may have left it.

I brought the wrapping to my nose, and instantly the scent of garlic and fresh bread sauntered into the air. My stomach grumbled a second time, and I unwrapped the gift ferociously. Inside the package was a fresh sandwich. Again, I looked around to see if anyone ran toward me, looking to retrieve their forgotten lunch. No one came. A moment later I shoved the sandwich into my mouth, barely allowing myself to breathe in between bites. I finished eating in record time and belched loudly.

A sneering mother with three young children scurried past my bench with a look of horror plastered across her done-up face.

"What? You've never seen a homeless guy eat before?" I called after her.

Bitch.

It's bad enough that sandwich may be my only fresh meal for the next week, then I gotta deal with judgmental yuppies? Bitterness boiled within me, and the taste in my mouth turned sour. If only she knew what I dealt with day in and day out. And, yeah, I get it. Some people see a homeless guy on the street and think he's just a bum who's too lazy to find a job. I wish laziness were my problem. Life would be so much easier if that were the case.

I stood from my bench and stretched my arms over my head. The frigid air shocked me. I knew it was time to take my daily walk around the city. What else did I have to do? I rolled my sleeping bag into a tight bunch like a frightened potato bug and hoisted it on my back.

If my calculations were correct, in another few days, it would be my turn to spend a few nights at the local homeless shelter. See, myself and the other guys on the streets had to take turns; the shelter only had so many beds. We rotated nights, and soon, I'd have a cot and a clean sheet to call my own, for a few days at least. During the day though, no matter what, I was on my own. The shelter only opened around meal times and for the select few at night. During the day, the building served as a center for AA meetings.

Once, I pretended to be an alcoholic so I could crash a meeting and have a complimentary donut and coffee. After a few meetings, the leader suspected I wasn't an addict at all. He politely asked me to leave after he caught me stuffing my jacket with angel cream pastries.

Was I lonely? Sure. Did I want the company? Not really. Relationships require communication, and the last thing I ever wanted to do was tell someone about my past. Sometimes, it's better to let sleeping dogs lie. Or, in my case, leave the bum alone.

Chapter Six

AMELIA

After lunch, I met with a potential client and spent the rest of the day pouring over my matters I brought with me from my last firm. Once I told a few of my corporate clients about my new job, they asked to remain clients of mine despite me switching to a new law office. Most of their work didn't require in-person meetings, and so I could work on their cases from any office I wanted.

While I highlighted a few sheets with a neon yellow highlighter, my phone rang and pulled me out of my concentration.

"Hello?" I answered.

"Mrs. Montgomery?"

"It's Ms., but yes, this is she."

"This is the principal over at Pinewood Elementary. The after school program ended a half hour ago, but no one has come to pick up Charlie. When can we expect you to arrive?"

Oh, fuck.

"Sorry, there must have been a miscommunication with our babysitter. I'll be there right away."

My heart plunged and guilt sucker-punched me in the gut. All the excitement of starting a new job distracted me from the most important job: being a mother. I locked my computer, grabbed my

coat and flew down the stairs where the cleaning crew was vacu-
uming and wiping down the surfaces in our lobby. I thrust open
the building doors and sprinted to my car, my coat still unzipped.

The school was a ghost town when I pulled in toward the cafeteria in the back of the brick building. Only three other cars
remained in the lot. I jogged the few yards from my car to the
back doors, my heels clacking the entire time.

I reached for the handle to open the door, only to find it was
securely locked. An audible groan erupted from my throat, and I
pounded on the doors. Charlie strutted toward the door with his
winter jacket tied around his petite waste and his Iron Man backpack bouncing along with him.

"Hey, kiddo!"

"Mom, it's a push door, not a pull," he said, his voice muffled.

I gawked at him incredulously, then tried to push the door.
This time, it opened with ease.

"Oh, yeah, I knew that. I was just testing you," I jested.

"Sure," he said and rolled his eyes.

Again, with the damn eye rolling!

"Ready to go home?"

The principal emerged from behind Charlie with his arms
crossed against his chest and pursed lips.

"Sorry again," I said to the principal.

He nodded, but his gaze never wavered. Shame washed over
me. Today, I was a stellar lawyer, but a shitty mom. I'd have to
make it up to Charlie somehow.

My son galloped to the car and jumped into the back seat
once I unlocked it with my fob. I started the engine and turned
the heat on full blast. "What do you think you want for dinner?"

"Pizza."

"How about something a little healthier?"

"White pizza." He turned on his iPad, which I kept in the
pouch attached to the back of the passenger seat, and tuned out
our conversation. I had to hand it to him, though. He was clever.

"Good one. What about a tasty chicken Caesar salad?"

"Nah," he answered.

"Fine, you win." I wasn't in the mood to cook, anyway, and a pizza sounded delicious. My mouth watered.

The problem? I still had no idea which places had quality food around here.

"Siri? Call the closest pizza shop."

"Calling Josie's Pizza, Wings and More," Siri said stoically.

I ordered a small white pizza and a large order of garlic bread. It had to be better than scraping up a last minute meal with the little ingredients I had at home.

A half hour later, Charlie and I sat at the table devouring our dinner. It would have been sooner, but I had to wrestle the iPad from his hands. Consequently, I grounded him for the rest of the night from the damn thing. Kids these days!

I rubbed my belly while Charlie burped obnoxiously loud. "Excuse me," he tittered.

I narrowed my eyes and tried to stifle my laugh. Sometimes I had the hardest time reprimanding my son when he acted out, especially when bodily functions were involved. I may be a lawyer, but I have a sense of humor too.

"How was school?" I questioned as I cleared the table.

"Fine."

"Just fine?"

"Yeah, Mom. It was just like a regular day."

"Did you make any friends?"

"A few," he said.

"Good!"

"Mom?"

"Yes, sweetie?"

"Did you forget about me again?"

My heart thudded with sadness. "I'm sorry, buddy. I lost track of time."

"You work too much," Charlie said.

I sighed. "Hey, why don't you go wash your hands?"

Charlie growled.

"Go!" I pointed toward the bathroom door down the hall.

"I just washed my hands before dinner!"

"Well, wash 'em again or no ice cream." Those three words were more powerful than any others I could muster with my kid. He had a sweet tooth, and sometimes, I used that to my advantage. Someone once told me the key to having your kids listen was to find out what they loved the most then threaten to take it away. I chuckled every time his eyes grew when I threatened to cancel dessert.

While Charlie busied himself in the bathroom, I retrieved the mail and sorted through the piles of junk and bills. One letter caught my eye with its Victorian script, and my heart plunged at rapid speed. I knew it was coming, but that didn't mean I was any more prepared. I ripped open the envelope, and consequently, a papercut seared across my finger. A few tears dripped down my cheeks while blood simultaneously dropped down my finger. I called out an expletive, which sent Charlie running from the bathroom back into the kitchen.

"Mama! Are you okay?"

Cursing under my breath this time, I answered, "Yes. Sorry, sweetie. Papercut."

Charlie shrugged and walked away. Apparently, a papercut meant nothing to him. I sucked the blood from the wound and put a bandage on it right away. Once it was all cleaned up, I dreaded going back to the piece of mail which prompted the papercut in the first place.

It was an invitation—and not just any invitation; it was an invite to my ex-husband's wedding. I cringed and swallowed the bile which had risen in my throat. In a million years, I never thought I'd have to choose chicken or steak at Cal's wedding. I had to go, though, right? I couldn't let him think I wasn't strong enough to watch him exchange vows with his new bride. Oh,

Angela. The tall, brunette with an ostentatious rack and a voluptuous body. She graduated from college a few years ago. Her youth was the cherry on top.

They met at a bar where she worked through her senior year at the state college outside of town. At first, I thought she was just a fling, but once I found out Cal had introduced her to Charlie without my consent, well, let's just say things got a little heated. I told Cal he had no right to make parenting decisions without me. He told me I had no say in who he dated or introduced to Charlie. We screamed at each other for almost an hour at his house, my old address, before Angela intervened and apologized. She admitted she was wrong to come into Charlie's life before having spoken to me first. I admired her courage to stand up to a fiery mama bear ready to draw blood, but I still wasn't happy with the situation. Now, I wasn't exactly elated to see her marry the man I thought I'd be buried next to one day.

Cal, or Calvin, and I met our junior year of college. He stood only a few inches taller than me and wore his dark brown hair very short. Cliché, I know. He majored in business; I majored in criminal justice. We were the power couple, the dangerous duo, the dream team. All our friends envied our relationship. I thought I met the man I'd spend the rest of my life with. We married soon after I turned 23, and a couple years later, I was pregnant. But just when our lives were supposed to be bursting with joy, everything came crashing down.

As an associate at a large firm, I often worked eighty hours a week. If I wanted to advance my career, that meant doing everything in my power to impress the partners. Often, that meant forgoing sleep, and if they asked me to jump, I replied, "How high?"

At first, Cal didn't mind, but as time wore on, he grew frustrated with my schedule. I only slowed down when I gave birth to Charlie, but even then, I worked from home. If I wanted to make it as a lawyer, I had to put in the time. Cal didn't understand, because at his job, he worked forty hours a week, max.

Then, once I made partner, my responsibilities only expanded. Cal turned impatient and annoyed with me, which resulted in petty fights when I *was* home. He told me he felt like a single father. I told him he was being ridiculous. Guilt slammed into me every time I checked the clock during a late night at the office and knew my boys were at home without. I wanted to be home with them, cuddled on the couch with a bowl of ice cream in my lap. But I knew in my heart, becoming a successful attorney would help my family in the long run. I wanted to provide for them. I wanted to save money for us all to go on lavish vacations to Disney and to the beach. I wanted to shower my son with love and presents. I wanted all the finer things in life and I wanted my family to have them, too.

It hurt me on the deepest of levels when Cal questioned my love for him and our son. There's no one in the entire world I loved more. I just also happened to love my job. Why couldn't I love both? It felt as though I was being pulled in two separate directions, tearing me apart in the process.

Giving birth to Charlie was the happiest day of my life. It'd been a tough delivery and I spent many hours in the hospital, but when I held him in my arms for the very first time, my entire world changed. I never knew I could love something so small with such an undeniable intensity. This little boy moved mountains inside my heart. I wanted to give him everything I never had, but that required dedication on my part. I also wanted to set an example that hard work pays off.

Cal was fortunate enough to grow up in a wealthy household. He skated through school and his father helped him find a job after graduation. I wasn't afford such luxuries. I wanted to balance out Cal's luck with my passion for being the best.

I didn't want to believe my perfect marriage was destructible, but the chinks in our armor weakened with every passing day. We weren't supposed to be like other couples. We were supposed to be better than them.

On the night of our eighth wedding anniversary, I ended up working late and crashing on the couch in my office. I had completely forgotten our dinner plans and worked well into the night on a case coming up for trial in the next few weeks. Even though I'd been the one to ask my mother- and father-in-law to watch Charlie for the night, our plans completely slipped my mind. Cal never forgave me for that night.

"You love your job more than you love me," he said the next day when I came home.

"That's not true, Cal."

"Do you even care about your family? You're never home!"

"Of course I care!"

"Prove it, Amelia." He challenged.

Cal's demeanor devolved into a distant, icy wall toward me after I missed our anniversary dinner. We only spoke to discuss Charlie, and even then, his voice was clipped and short. I tried to cut my hours short at work from time to time, but even then, Cal wanted me home even more.

Every weekend for the next few months, I made an effort to plan a family outing. One Saturday, we went to the zoo, another I bought tickets for the local science museum. However, if I checked my phone or responded to an email while we were out, Cal shot me contemptuous looks. It felt like it was never enough for him.

I wished more than anything he understood the demands of working in a law firm. I wished he knew every night I spent at the office, I wished I could be with them, too. I begged him to realize that every day I came home early, I lost the opportunity to succeed.

I couldn't keep up the facade any longer, though and neither could he. Cal began sleeping in our guest bedroom, if he came home at all. Our nanny sensed the disarray in our home, despite my attempts to conceal our imminent demise.

One evening, Cal came home and rushed into the shower after throwing his clothes in the washer. Suspicion rippled through me as I tiptoed to the laundry room, opened the washer and pulled out Cal's sopping button-up shirt. On the collar, bright red lipstick was smeared across the material.

Most wives would have been overcome with devastation. Me, however, I was relieved. This was my "out." Sure, it hurt to know he was sleeping with another woman, but now I wouldn't have to endure his endless rants about my work hours and lack of dedication to our marriage.

I cornered him before bed and asked if he was having an affair. His reaction? He sighed, and a look of apathy enveloped his face. At one time, we were hopelessly in love. But our love spoiled over time, and the end seemed inevitable.

He admitted to having an affair with Angela, the bartender. We divorced several months later and BAM, I became a single mother in the blink of an eye. I never thought it would happen to me. I never imagined I'd struggle to find babysitters or have to bring my child to work with me on days a sitter wasn't available. I shouldered the brunt of parenthood while Cal took Charlie on the weekends and went public with his new relationship. My world collapsed around me, but I couldn't wallow in self-pity. I had a child to raise and a career to grow. Who knew it would take a divorce for me to cut down my hours at work? I still put in almost 60 hours a week, but I worked far less than what I used to.

Last year, the scars of divorce still fresh, I heard it through the grapevine that Cal proposed to Angela. I knew he'd shacked up with her, but marriage? We'd only been divorced around two years. It was when I ran into them one night at a cozy Italian restaurant, I realized the rumors were true. I saw the way he watched Angela, and my heart shattered. He looked at her the way he once looked at me:

deeply and utterly in love. Not to mention, the ring on her finger glittered in the dim light of the restaurant. I couldn't prevent the pang of jealousy from crashing into me when I realized the diamond was far larger than the one Cal bought me so many years ago.

Even though it was for the best, and our marriage wouldn't have lasted, a piece of my heart died the night I realized Cal moved on. Would I ever be granted my own chance to move on? Would I ever find someone who accepted both my love and dedication to my job?

Now, with the invitation in hand, I had to decide whether or not to attend my ex-husband's wedding.

Fuck me.

Chapter Seven

AMELIA

My first week of work flew by. Friday morning arrived, and I struggled to motivate Charlie to dress as usual. I swear moms who don't lose their shit by the end of the day deserve an award. Especially single moms. Hell, forget the prize; I'd settle for a sweet cookie instead.

"Charlie, move your tush, or else I'm taking the iPad away for a week!"

A massive crash erupted from his bedroom, and I knew my threat put a fire under him, as I hoped it would. I stood in the kitchen with Charlie's lunch bag in tow, along with my purse draped over my shoulder and my new cozy cashmere scarf wrapped around my neck.

I swore at the television as the weatherman promised temperatures in the teens for today.

Damn, I hated winter.

Why couldn't my firm be in Florida or California? I sighed as I dreamt about warmer days and prayed winter would pass swiftly this year.

"I'm ready, Mom!" Charlie scrambled from his Star Wars bedroom and skidded to a halt before me.

"Did you brush your hair?"

He nodded.

"And, your teeth?"

"Yes! Now let's get on the road before you make us late." Charlie chuckled, and I rolled my eyes. He was growing up way too fast. What would I do when he grew up, though? If the sass began at nine, what would the kid be like at nineteen? I shuddered at the thought.

I shook away my thoughts about my only child becoming a man and glanced around as I tried to think if I was forgetting anything. The apartment was in better shape every day, but we still had a lot of work to do. I knew if I worked less, I'd have more time to clean the place up, but I couldn't see that happening any time soon.

The ivory walls were recently painted, and the chestnut hardwood floors sparkled in the daylight. The living room windows spanned the length of one wall, which revealed a stunning view of the city. The apartment was spacious without being obnoxious. Charlie and I were comfortable and at ease in our new digs.

Once I assured myself I wasn't forgetting anything I needed for the day, Charlie and I headed down to the complex's private parking ramp. Charlie hopped into the backseat of the car and held out his hand expectantly.

"How may I help you?" I taunted as I started the car.

"C'mon, Mom! I was ready when you asked me to be!"

"But, how many times did I have to ask?"

Charlie lowered his head, and I couldn't help but snicker. It was far too easy to trick that kid. I handed him his iPad and drove toward his school.

"Are you ready for your spelling test today?" I inquired as we turned the corner, his school now in view.

"Oh yeah. I'm going to make you proud, Mama," Charlie promised while he played his game. I smiled when his tongue fell slightly out of his mouth. It was his "concentration" face.

"Well, I can't wait to hear all about it," I said. "Okay, bud. We're here."

Charlie moaned but did a few last second things with his game. I assumed he was saving his progress and turning it off. He handed it to me as he stretched from the backseat closer to me.

"Love you," he said and kissed my cheek.

My heart fluttered, and I wished him a good day at school. No matter how old Charlie grew, there was nothing better than a kiss and hug from my baby. He'd always be my baby, even when he stood taller than me someday.

I watched and made sure he made it into the building all right and pulled out of the commuter circle. A few other moms waved awkwardly toward me, and I returned the favor with a half-smile. I'd been asked to join the PTA once Charlie transferred, as if I had free time to spare. Most nights, after Charlie went to bed, I pored over open cases with a glass of wine. It was always hard to disconnect from work even when I was home. I guess it was better to focus on my clients' problems than worry about my own.

I glanced at the temperature on my dashboard and winced. I'm pretty sure humans weren't meant to live in a place where the air hurt their faces. Sighing heavily, another thought popped into my mind: what would the homeless man be doing on a day like this? Would the shelter open for emergencies? Surely he could find a place to rest until the air warmed up a bit?

My chest seized as I wondered about the man. I thought about what I could do to help. Could I give him money? But, then again, what if he used it for drugs or booze or something? I mean, he seemed innocent enough, but you never really knew these days.

A familiar green sign came into view while I drove through the snow and the slush. I quickly flicked my signal and turned into the Starbucks parking lot. Maybe an appetizing hot chocolate would be the appropriate gesture for him. It couldn't hurt to try, right?

I ordered a grande espresso with a vanilla flavor shot and a venti hot chocolate for the man without a home. If I could bring him a few moments of warmth for the day, well, that would be something—and better than nothing.

Once I pulled out of the Starbucks lot, my office was only a short drive away. I reached my designated parking lot and braced myself for the swoosh of frigid air about to bitch-slap me in the face. I closed my eyes and stepped out of the car with both drinks in a recyclable paper carrier. I tiptoed through the snow and cursed the owners of the lot for not plowing yet.

Fuck, fuck, fuck!

Then, I cursed myself for not buying the tall Uggs on Black Friday because the shorties weren't cutting it at all; my ankles were soaked and frozen. I couldn't catch a damn break!

As I approached the bench, I wasn't sure if I wanted him to be there or not. If he wasn't there, then I'd spend the rest of the day worrying about where he could be and if he was safe. If he was there, well, then I'd still spend the rest of the day worrying about him too. I didn't quite understand my fascination with the man. I mean, that sleeping bag isn't some kind of antique. I'm sure tons of other people have the same one. All I knew was that it didn't appear like anyone else gave a shit about him. Maybe I could be the one person who did?

My hands quivered either with nerves or because of the cold. The bench stood a hundred yards away, and the sleeping man snoozed away at his post. His beard appeared long and flowing. I wondered when the last time he shaved was? His tattered, burgundy sleeping bag was zipped all the way to his neck as he lay inside of it on the bench, under a tree with breathtaking snowflakes hugging its branches.

My pace slowed, and my heart thudded through my shirt. What would I say? Should I say anything at all? What if he didn't want to be disturbed? What if he didn't like hot chocolate?

Those thoughts and more raced through my head as doubt

and second thoughts crept into my mind. Without me realizing it, my feet carried me close enough to touch the man. His eyes remained shut, and I peeked over my shoulder to see if anyone had caught me standing over him. Fortunately, everyone seemed too self-absorbed and busy on their phones to notice.

I looked down at the man, and my breath caught in my throat. He was young, probably around my age if not a few years shy. I don't know what I expected, but I didn't think the man would be my peer instead of my elder. How did this happen to him?

Without warning, the man opened his eyes and gasped as he saw me standing less than a foot away, hovering over him. His swift movement caught me off guard as I cried out and accidentally tossed the Starbucks drinks into the air in fright.

I knew what was coming, and there was nothing I could do to stop it. The steaming hot coffee and hot chocolate rained down upon my head. I screeched again as the liquid seared my skin and drenched me from head to foot.

Freaking gravity!

I yelped in pain, and the homeless man sat up straight, still cocooned in his sleeping bag. He cleared his throat and spoke. "Are you, uh, okay?"

My cheeks reddened as I cleared my throat. "I'm fine. Just embarrassed."

The man eyed me carefully, his gaze wild and alarmed.

"My name is Amelia," I said weakly.

"William," he said. "What are you doing over here, anyway?"

"Well, I, uh, I've seen you around, and I thought you could use some hot chocolate. It's fucking cold out." I internally chided myself for swearing like a damn sailor.

"Oh," he said.

Great, now I'd embarrassed him. I stared awkwardly at my boots and sighed. "I'm sorry." I didn't know what else to say. My good deed of the day failed miserably.

"Thank you for the hot chocolate," William whispered.

"Can I take you to lunch?" I blurted out.

This time, William blushed. "No..."

"Please? I'd like to make up for my epic fail."

"No, thank you."

"I honestly don't mind," I chirped optimistically.

"I'm tired. Go away," William breathed.

He peered into my eyes, and I examined his face for the first time. A faint sparkle of the man he used to be shone through the wear and tear.

I could also see the pain etched on his face. His cheeks were sunken in, and I caught the haunted expression looking back at me. I wanted to hug him, to pull him into my arms and save him. Whenever I thought about homeless men before, I assumed they were all older, that they'd die on the streets. But, this guy? He had his entire life ahead of him. He shouldn't be out here. I reminded myself of a child, eager to take home a stray dog.

"I'm sorry for bothering you."

He glanced away and laid back down on the bench with his back to me.

I guess that meant the conversation was over. I left his side without a goodbye and wallowed the rest of the way to my office. I wanted more than anything to help William, but I knew I couldn't help someone who didn't want to accept it.

Chapter Eight

AMELIA

"Good morning and happy Friday, Amelia!" Ross said as he stepped into my office. "You survived your first week."

"Hi, Ross." I smiled.

"How are you feeling? Did you get a chance to look over the case?"

"I'm feeling, no, I *am* very confident, sir. I spent a lot of time this week preparing." I wasn't exaggerating, either. I studied the case notes every single day this week during breakfast, on my lunch break and even before bed. I knew it cold. I knew it like the back of my hand.

It didn't appear too complicated. Leo Brass Incorporated, a substantial construction firm in the city, believed their chief accountant, Roy Franko, was skimming profits and hiding them in offshore accounts. Leo wanted to hire a firm to take Roy to civil court and sue him for the missing funds. My job was to prove to Leo, the founder, president, and CEO, that I could establish Roy was, in fact, stealing money and hiding it elsewhere. I didn't usually handle civil court matters, but Leo was a major client of the firm's, and handling his case would be a way to get my feet wet at the new office.

It would take a lot of legwork and a pinch of detective work, too. We'd have to hire a private investigator and also an impartial accountant to look over the company's books and numbers. I read in the file that Leo hadn't gone to the police yet; he didn't want the story to leak to the press or have it tried in criminal court proceedings. At least not yet, anyway.

"We're meeting in Conference Room B in about fifteen. See you there!" Ross waved and scurried out of my office.

I took a deep breath, gathered my notes and the case file, and finished the last dregs of my French vanilla latte, which I purchased at the cafeteria since I threw the first one all over myself. Coffee grounds permeated the air around me, but I hoped nobody would notice.

I'd worn my best outfit today: tight, yet professional, black pencil skirt, matching blazer and a sheer white button up top underneath. I also donned a pearl necklace and earrings for an extra touch of chic. I thanked myself for investing in the teeth whitening treatment back home before I moved because it allowed me to sport a bold cherry-red lipstick without my self-esteem crashing down.

I stood and smoothed my outfit one last time as I departed my office and headed toward the conference room. Thankfully, only my coat was soaked this morning. My outfit survived that embarrassment.

Leo Brass seized a spot at the large marble conference table. He stood as I entered the room, and a broad smile stretched across his face.

"You must be the famous Amelia Montgomery I've heard so much about."

My cheeks reddened to the color of my lipstick as I extended my hand toward him. "Pleasure to meet you, sir. I hope you've only heard the good things about me."

"All good things, I promise!" A hearty chuckle erupted from his rotund belly.

At around fifty years old, Leo still appeared handsome. I could tell, though, at one time he was probably the fire in every woman's loins. His salt and pepper hair lay cleanly styled, and his crystal clear cerulean eyes sparkled. He was the perfect business-man: handsome, charismatic and genuine.

I only hoped I could wow him more than any other attorney so he'd hire us to take on his case.

"Can I get you water, coffee?"

He raised his water glass. "I'm all set, but thank you, Amelia."

I sat down in a comfy leather chair across from Leo. The conference rooms in the office screamed prestige with awards covering the walls and beautifully painted portraits of various attorneys spread about.

"So, you just moved here, if I'm not mistaken?"

"Yes, sir. About a month ago."

"How do you like our city so far?"

"It's been an adjustment; I won't deny that. But, so far so good."

"How do you like the firm?"

"Well, it's much bigger than my last firm, but I'm already in love." I wasn't sure if he was genuinely interested or probing for details. However, I didn't need to embellish; I really did love it here so far.

"Happy to hear that!"

Then, Ross stepped into the room with a jovial expression and arms extended. Leo stood again, and the two men embraced each other like long-lost friends.

"Leo! How are you?"

"I'm good, but I'll be even better once you prove to me you can handle my case."

"You're in amazing hands, my friend. I see you've met Amelia, our star attorney?"

"You've got one hell of a woman on your hands," Leo said, glowing.

I blushed again. I wasn't used to such high praise, especially from men in my field. At my last firm, I was looked down upon almost as if I were the secretary. I think some men couldn't handle my intelligence. At least, that's what I told myself after a particularly stressful day.

"Shall we get down to business?" Ross proposed.

"Absolutely," Leo concurred.

I cleared my throat and stood before both men as I began the opening statement of my presentation.

"Leo, first I'd like to say thank you for considering Logan and Logan Attorneys at Law. We understand your need for privacy and the desire to meet a speedy conclusion in your matter. We are grateful you are considering entrusting us with your case, and we promise to meet and exceed any and all expectations you may have. We also know there are other firms bidding for your business, but we assure you, Logan and Logan is your best bet when it comes to recovering your missing income and prosecuting the man or people involved to the fullest extent of the law."

I went into a little more about my background and explained my history with high-profile cases. Bragging a little, I also detailed my win/loss ratio, which was phenomenal.

Leo and Ross's respective gazes stayed fixed on me during my entire presentation, and the intensity of their stares only fueled my desire to land the case. I laid it all out on the table and promised a favorable outcome for Leo Brass Incorporated, even though attorneys shouldn't make promises. However, confidence bloomed inside of me like a flower at the beginning of spring.

I concluded my speech and held my breath as Leo opened his mouth to speak. "Ms. Montgomery, you are something else. I'd like to sign a contract to work with you immediately."

Relief and exhilaration washed over my body as I broke out into a jubilant grin. "That's excellent, sir! I am so happy to hear that."

Ross clapped Leo on the back. "Happy to work with you again, my friend. I'll have the paperwork drawn up right away."

I felt like a giddy little girl who received a pony for her birthday. I was only at the law firm for a week when I scored my first big case. This fresh start thing was looking less scary by the minute. I was slightly taken aback that Leo decided to hire us on the spot, but I assumed other firms failed to provide an impressive speech as I had done.

Back in my office, Ross first knocked, then burst into the room. "You were excellent, Amelia! This is going to be huge for our firm!"

"I'm happy it went so well, too."

"We are so lucky to have you here. And, I'm happy I bugged you persistently until you accepted my offer."

I rolled my eyes and chuckled. "I'm happy, too. Although, I don't think my old firm was too happy about you stealing me away."

Ross returned my smile. "Leo wants to take us out for dinner next week to celebrate."

"Sounds good. I can't wait!"

"Laurie is drawing up the paperwork now, and I'll have her bring it up to you shortly to sign. I also have her come up with a list of PI's and freelance accountants to help with the case. Of course, you will have final say on anyone we hire."

"Perfect," I said.

"Well done, Amelia. I have a good feeling about this one."

"Me, too, sir."

Me, too.

Chapter Nine

WILLIAM

On my eighteenth birthday, my father was murdered. He died in the attack on the World Trade Center. I'd never see him again. I'd never hear his laugh or his cries. I'd never hug him or shake his hand. He'd never see me graduate from college or be there on my wedding day. He'd never see the birth of my children. My father's life was stolen, and the terrorists robbed my family and so many others of a lifetime of happiness.

After the initial shock wore off, my body flooded with fury. I didn't cry; I didn't weep. I didn't even mourn my father. Instead, I wanted revenge. I wanted blood. I wanted to kill.

I spent the next few months in a daze of anger and hatred. I stopped going to class, stopped eating, stopped sleeping. But I couldn't stop thinking about my father's last few moments on Earth. Did he die happy? Did he feel any pain? All I knew for sure was that my father died a loved man. He was my best friend, and I cared about him more than anything.

Would I ever repair the gaping wound left by his absence? Would I ever recover? I didn't think so. I didn't think it would be possible to mend this kind of broken heart. I couldn't contain my rage. I exploded and snapped at anyone and everyone.

On the other end of the grief spectrum, my mother almost never left the bedroom. I did my best to take care of her, and to be honest, I had the time since I'd forgone taking care of myself. She was numb to reality, yet felt it strongly all at once. The light left her eyes, and she wasn't living; she merely existed. She took an extended leave of absence from work, and I feared she'd never go back.

At school, my advisor suggested I take the rest of the semester off. He said I could use the break from school to grieve, and I still had time to back out of my classes without failing and tarnishing my GPA.

I gladly took my advisor's advice and spent the rest of the semester at home with my mother. However, I knew I couldn't stay home forever and owed it to my father to graduate from college, as he always wished I would.

The next couple of years passed in a daze. I managed to pass all my classes, but just barely. I treaded water, barely staying afloat. Between taking care of my mother and classes, I didn't have time for much else. Eventually, I graduated with a Bachelor's Degree in Business, but I had no idea how I'd use the piece of paper in the real world. Sure, there had to be dozens of opportunities in New York, but part of me couldn't imagine working in a stuffy office from nine to five every day.

On September 11th, 2006, the fifth anniversary of the attack, I went to the Army recruiting center and enlisted.

For the first time since my father died, I regained some semblance of control. I decided to do something meaningful in my life. I found the direction I needed to survive.

The day I came home to tell my mom about my decision may have been the second most devastating day of my life.

"Mom?" I asked timidly as I stepped into her bedroom.

Even though the clock read three in the afternoon, she still hadn't gotten out of bed or eaten yet.

"Hi, William," she uttered.

"I have something to talk to you about. It's important."

"Mhmmm?"

I sat on her bed and realized she hadn't washed the sheets since before dad died. I could smell the faint aroma of him lingering in the bedding. I *closed my eyes, inhaled and wished I could remember the way he smelled forever.*

"I'm joining the military," I said.

"That's nice, dear."

I sighed. "Mom? Did you hear me? I'm going to fight for our country. I'm going to fight for Dad."

She peered at me with fresh eyes. "You're leaving?"

Her gaze pierced my heart, and I realized how much this would hurt her. She lost her husband, and now she was "losing" her only child.

"I enlisted in the Army. I need to do something meaningful with my life, and I think this is it."

"You're leaving school?" She stared out of the window.

"I already graduated, Ma. Remember you came to my ceremony in the spring? I start basic training in two weeks."

"That's soon," she answered absently.

"I love you, Mom. I want you to know that. I'll never stop loving you."

"I miss him."

I hung my head and took a deep breath to steady myself. "I miss him, too."

"I'm going to be all alone now."

My heart ached for my mother, but I knew I had to do this. I had to leave. I couldn't stay in this brownstone and go to work like nothing ever happened. Everything was different now. Nothing would ever be the same. In fact, if I stayed, she'd probably "lose" me sooner. For the first time in years, I felt a sense of hope and purpose. If I stayed, I knew I'd continue on the path to self-destruction.

"I promise I'll call as often as I can. And I'll write you, too. Okay?"

She nodded, but I could tell she'd lost all interest in the conversation. I bent down, kissed her cheek and went downstairs to make a phone call.

"Uncle Jim? It's William. I was hoping I could ask you for a favor."

My father's brother Jimmy was a great uncle and spoiled me as much as he could. He'd taken me fishing for the first time, gave me advice on girls, and even slipped me my first beer. Even though my father was the number one man in my life, my Uncle Jimmy was a solid number two.

"Well, I was hoping you might be able to come stay with my mom for a little while. I'm going away, and she needs someone to take care of her. She's in rough shape. Where am I going? Um, well, I'm going into the Army."

Silence impregnated the conversation. I knew my uncle was processing what I'd just told him. However, a moment later he told me he'd do whatever he could to help and that he was genuinely proud of me. I sighed heavily with his blessing in mind, and also because he said he would come that weekend to get settled and spend time with me before I left.

My uncle, a widower, never remarried. He was several years older than my father and retired when he turned fifty-five. Must be gratifying to be a successful financial adviser for thirty-plus years, huh?

Uncle Jimmy arrived as promised that weekend. I begged my mom to at least shower and get dressed before he came. I bought some groceries, at least enough to cook a decent meal with. Jitters rumbled in my belly as I waited for my uncle.

Once I heard the knock, I leaped up from the couch and raced to the door. When I threw it open, Uncle Jimmy stood on the doorstep with a broad grin stretched across his face.

He pulled me into a tight embrace, and without thinking, I began to sob into his chest. My father and Uncle Jimmy looked so similar; I thought my father stood before me for just a single moment. Having Uncle Jimmy here comforted me beyond all measures of the word.

That night, I made a simple chicken and pasta bake. My mother joined us for dinner and even managed to put on a touch of makeup. I hadn't seen her so put together since before the attack. We spent all evening sipping wine and tossing around the good memories of my father. Maybe it was possible to overcome my grief.

Maybe.

Chapter Ten
AMELIA

As soon as three o'clock rolled around, I realized I'd been cruising on the high from the morning for so long, I'd forgotten to eat lunch. Regrettably, the cafe in the office closed, so I needed to figure out something else to eat.

I remembered there was a cute little cafe tucked in the middle of a handful of offices down the block. I checked their website and saw they closed at four. I had just enough time to scurry down there and have a late lunch before I finished my work for the day and headed to pick up Charlie.

Grabbing my coat, I tucked my phone into the pocket and wrapped my scarf snuggly around my neck. The weatherman pissed me off again today when he promised more frigid temperatures that would last until the weekend.

I grabbed the elevator on my floor before its doors closed, heaving a sigh of relief once I realized no one else was in the car. I hated elevators and their mandatory awkwardness. I mean, what do you say when you're in a tight space with a stranger? Usually, I pray my coffee breath won't knock them out—or hope I remembered to put on deodorant in the morning.

Once I reached the first floor, I smiled at the guard and

stepped outside. The air assaulted my face, and for a moment, I regretted moving here at all. Then, I remembered the feeling this morning when Leo said he'd chosen us as the firm to represent him. It made the cold air sting a little less, but just a little bit.

I spotted the cafe, Your Cup of Tea, a short distance away, and trudged through the snow and slush toward the brick building. With my hood and scarf bundled up around me, I'd lost my peripheral vision. I could only see straight ahead.

Without warning, my stiletto heel caught in the crack of the sidewalk as I swayed, ready to fall flat on my ass. But someone caught me and broke my fall just in time. I whipped around and stood nose to nose with none other than William. His eyes pierced my soul, and my heart attempted to leap out of my chest.

"William!"

"Oh, it's you again," he said casually.

Blushing for the hundredth time that day, I swallowed hard. "Thank you."

I stood up straight of my own accord, smoothing out my coat. My subconscious screamed so loudly at me, I couldn't ignore it any longer. "Will you have lunch with me?"

William raised his eyebrows. "You speak English, lady? I already told you no."

"But I'm just going to the cafe down the street, and I'd love some company."

He was about to decline again; I could tell by the sadness etched into his face.

"Pretty please?"

His gaze softened, and he glanced around. Barely any pedestrians walked the streets. After all, it was still business hours and well past lunch break. Not to mention it was freaking cold out!

"Well, I could use a hot meal," he trailed off.

I grinned broadly, excitement swooping in my stomach.

We walked in silence toward the cafe, where he held the door open for me once we reached its frosty glass door.

"Thank you."

He nodded as he stepped inside behind me. His stench swirled in the air, and I held my breath.

The cafe was cozy and quaint, but precisely what I wanted. Local artwork covered the walls, and smooth jazz crooned from the speakers. Not many people sat at the bamboo tables, but the staff was hustling and bustling behind the counter anyway.

A barista called from the cash register, telling us to sit wherever we liked. Her gaze stopped briefly on William, and while I caught her stare, I hoped he hadn't. The last thing I wanted was him to regret joining me for lunch because some teen couldn't keep her eyes to herself.

"Have you ever been here before?" I questioned curiously.

He furrowed his brows and shook his head.

Duh, Amelia. Don't be so awkward.

"It's my first time, too. What do you think you're in the mood for?"

We sat at a table away from the window, William's choosing. A beautiful cityscape painting hung on the wall next to us. The subtle strokes of pastel acrylics blew my mind. Damn, my new city was pretty.

William continued to study the menu. I wondered what was going through his head. Was he afraid to order? Did he even want anything from this place?

"I'm thinking about a panini," I said, hoping to break the impenetrable silence.

"Me, too," he replied.

The timid waitress popped over to our table with a couple of waters and notepad at the ready to take our orders. We both ordered the steak and mozzarella panini. I noticed the waitress wouldn't make eye contact with either of us. I couldn't technically blame her. I'm sure the scene was confusing: a professional woman in a suit eating lunch with a man wearing two winter coats and a beard that would rival Forrest Gump's.

Once she walked away rather hurriedly, I drew a blank as what to say next. What exactly do you talk to a homeless man about?

I settled on an easy one, or so I hoped. "So, where are you from?"

"New York City," he said. Reluctantly, he took off his winter coats and wiped a bead of sweat from his brow.

"What a great city!"

William shrugged. "It's okay."

"I'm from Candlebrook," I said. "Not too far from Pittsburgh."

He nodded but didn't respond.

Fuck, this is isn't going well.

"What brought you here?"

"You're nosey."

"Well, I'd just like to get to know you is all." I shrugged.

"But why?"

I hesitated. "Well, to be honest, you kind of remind me of my father."

William grunted. "Your dad was a bum, too?"

I swallowed. "No, but he had the same sleeping bag as you, and he was also in the military."

William reached for his dog tags, clutching them in his gritty fingertips.

"Which branch?" I asked.

"Army."

"Thank you for your service, William."

He nodded and finished his Coke.

"I bet you have a lot of stories from your time in the military," I offered enthusiastically.

Again, he nodded with no response. Maybe I shouldn't pry? Maybe something bad happened to him while serving?

The waitress returned with our paninis, a welcome interruption to our conversation, which seemed to be going nowhere.

My mouth watered as I glanced down at my plate. Out of the

corner of my eye, I saw William's eyes grow two sizes bigger. I wondered if it was the first warm meal he'd had in a long time. Well, at least since I left him the sandwich. Elation bloomed in my chest as I felt happy to be the one providing it to him.

"This looks so good! Almost too good to eat!"

I peered up to William and saw he'd dug into his panini. A piece of mozzarella cheese dangled from his lip, caught in his beard.

I smiled, took my napkin, and reached to pull the cheese off his mouth. He flinched at my touch, which in turn, caused me to pull back. If anyone were watching us, they'd either be laughing or feeling fucking sad. We'd certainly be the most awkward people they'd ever seen.

"Sorry," I said, shrugging.

"Whatever."

I ate half my panini, and while I could have finished the other half, I saw William's eyes stare at the savory steak and cheese on my plate. "I'm full; do you want the rest of mine?"

"No, thank you."

I shook my head and scraped the rest of my lunch onto his plate. "Eat," I demanded.

Without waiting for his protest, I stood and went to the ladies' room to freshen up. I walked into the restroom, reapplied my lipstick and put an extra glob of concealer under my eyes. The bags under my soft chestnut-brown eyes were far too noticeable for my liking. I needed to get more sleep.

I walked back into the central part of the cafe and heard fierce arguing erupt over by the table William and I had chosen.

A man in a chef's hat stood berating William, whose fists were clutched at his sides.

"No loitering! You must leave this instant!"

William stood, his eyes narrowed and his chest heaving. "I'm not loitering, asshole."

The man, whom I assumed to be the manager, yelled back, "Leave now, or I'll call the police."

I rushed to the table and tapped on the manager's shoulder. "Excuse me, but what is going on here?"

The manager, old enough to be my father, huffed and puffed. He looked at me and back to William several times. "This man is homeless. We are not a homeless shelter."

William took a step toward the manager, but I held my arm out to prevent his advance.

"My name is Amelia Montgomery. I'm with Logan and Logan Attorneys at Law. This gentleman is my guest for lunch. He is not loitering, and if you'd like, we can settle this back at my office."

The manager's eyes grew, then he spewed apologies. I held up my hand, indicating for him to stop talking. I turned back to look at William, except he was gone. He'd vanished without a sound. All that he'd left behind was a crumpled five dollar bill.

I grabbed my coat, ignored the manager's continued apologies, and stalked out of the cafe. I looked up and down the block, but William was nowhere to be seen.

Just when I'd convinced him to take a chance and join me for lunch, everything blew up in my face. The high I rode from the morning evaporated, and nausea forced itself upon me. This man, a war veteran no less, didn't deserve that kind of treatment.

I wondered deep down if I'd ever see him again. And, if I did, would he even want to talk to me?

Fuck.

Chapter Eleven

AMELIA

Later that evening, Charlie's father, Cal, arrived at our apartment to pick him up. Part of the custody agreement said he was able to take Charlie for extended breaks during the school year. Charlie's school would let out Monday for February break, and starting today, for the next two weeks, I'd have the apartment to myself. As much of a handful as my darling son could be, when we were apart, it felt like a piece of me was missing. This would be the first time in our lives Charlie would be so far away from me. Candlebrook was three hours away. He might as well be a whole world away.

Once I heard the knock at the front door, my stomach dropped. I never looked forward to seeing my ex-husband, but the smug look on his face when I opened the door stirred my rage.

"Cal," I said, not trying to hide my distaste.

"Amelia."

I stood in the doorway and called to Charlie. "Your father's here."

"Coming!" Charlie replied excitedly. I knew I should be happy he'd have the opportunity to spend time with his father, but did he have to sound so pleased about it? Ugh.

"So, are you going to let me in?" Cal asked.

"Sure." I stepped aside and let him come in.

I crossed my arms over my chest and secretly wished I hadn't thrown on yoga pants and a ratty college tee shirt as soon as I'd gotten home.

"Did you get the invitation?"

"You mean the invitation to your wedding?"

"Uh, yeah."

"I did."

"Are you going to come?" He asked carefully.

"I'm not sure yet. I'll have to check my work schedule."

Cal nodded and rolled his eyes. "I see things haven't changed much. Charlie, c'mon kid. We have a long drive back!"

Charlie cruised down the hallway with his backpack resting firmly on his shoulders. "Ready, Dad!"

I pulled my son into a deep bear hug and squeezed him until he cried out. "Hun fun, okay?"

"Duh, Mom. Dad and I always have fun."

"You can Facetime me anytime. Day or night. I'll make sure to have my phone on me. And call me if you need anything."

"Mellie, it's just two weeks," Cal muttered.

I shot him a scathing glance. I hated that nickname, and he knew it. "I know how long he will be gone, Cal."

"Okay, guys," Charlie interrupted. "I love you, Mom. I'll make sure to keep in touch."

I kissed him on the forehead and gave him one last hug. "I love you, sweetheart."

"Love you too!"

And, just like that, my baby was off to Candlebrook. I leaned against the door and slid down to the floor. I missed him already. What would I do for two whole weeks without him? After a few minutes sulking in my pity party, I pulled myself up and headed toward the wine rack. Maybe a cold glass of Pinot Grigio would lighten my mood. It was going to be a long two weeks without my buddy.

A few attorneys from work invited me out tonight, but I politely declined. With Charlie gone, I wanted to spend a little more time on a few more potential client pitches.

By eleven o'clock, I'd hit a snag in my research as I realized I left an important file on my desk. I groaned and cursed myself. Sure, I could stop working and go to bed; the file and research would be waiting for me on Monday. Not to mention, my proposal wasn't due for another week, but I loved having my work completed ahead of time.

I paced the apartment, biting my nails to the quick. *What to do, what to do?*

Groaning, I shuffled to the kitchen and retrieved my purse and my keys. I wobbled to the door as the wine hit me all at once. There was no way I could drive like this, which also meant I shouldn't be working with a buzz, either.

Regardless, I ordered a Lyft to take me to work.

I grabbed my coat, ignoring my less-than-casual ensemble, and leaped down the apartment building stairs to the lobby. The building, erected in the 1920s, glowed with historic architecture. There's no way I would have been able to afford something like this at my old firm, but with my new position came a new, much larger salary.

I saw a white Escape parked out front, so I waved to my doorman as I jogged outside. My driver stayed quiet for the ride, which I felt eternally grateful for. I wasn't much of a talker, and I was also tipsy. Didn't want to make a fool of myself in front of a stranger. Once we arrived at my office building, I thanked him and wished him a good night.

With my ID badge in hand, I unlocked my firm's front doors and shivered as they clicked open. While some lights stayed on overnight, the building stood mostly in darkness. I wasn't a fan of horror movies, and the scene mirrored a slasher film. I dashed up the stairs, too frightened to take the elevator, and thanked God my office was only on the third floor. Several beads of sweat collected on my forehead and dribbled down my back. I flung my office door open and swished my hand in front of the motion-activated light. Once the fluorescent lights broke through the darkness, I squinted and willed my eyes to search for the file I needed.

There you are!

I grabbed the file and gazed outside my office windows to admire the gorgeous cityscape, brilliantly gleaming under the night sky. I smiled and put my hand to the glass, grateful I took this position in such a wonderful city.

A few dings interrupted my thoughts, and I looked down at my phone. I must have put my phone on silent by accident. I had a voicemail and missed a text from Charlie. Without reading the message or listening to the voicemail, I called him back right away.

"Hi, this is C-Dog. Leave a message, playa!"

I rolled my eyes and made a mental note to ask Cal what he was letting Charlie watch on television. I tried one more time, but he still didn't answer. I checked his text to me which read, "Goin to da movies. Bye!"

I missed my son more than anything, but now I'd have to wait until tomorrow to talk to him. Life can be lonely when you're leaning on just one person for balance. Good thing I had plenty of work to do to keep myself busy and distracted.

I'd temporarily forgotten my fear of whatever may lurk in the darkness of the building as I moped down the stairs to the foyer and out into the night. I ordered another Lyft, and the app promised a driver would arrive in less than five minutes, but after ten passed, and no one showed up, annoyance seeped in.

I noticed a car parked a block away with its flashers blinking rapidly. Maybe the driver missed the address? I huffed and puffed like the big bad wolf as I trudged toward the car. Then, a group of rowdy twenty-somethings stumbled into the SUV I'd assumed was my ride. Guess not.

My eager footsteps echoed down the street as dozens of other drunk people walked in droves to the bars in the party district. I passed an alleyway where a stray kitten pawed against the restaurant door nearly hidden in the dark passageway. I tiptoed toward the tiny feline. The breeze chilled me to my core, and an eerie feeling flooded my consciousness as I approached the cat.

Something didn't feel right. I peeked over my shoulder and saw a man wearing all black, standing in the entrance of the alley. I hadn't noticed him at first. His head hung low, and he wore a black cap pulled right to his eyes. My heart thudded in my chest, and I wished I'd brought my pepper spray with me. Or that I hadn't gone down a dark alley on a Friday night by myself.

The man strode closer to me, his echoed footsteps bouncing off the buildings on either side of us. Despite the chill in the air, sweat dripped down the small of my back. The buzz from the wine vanished, replaced with sheer terror. I heard the man clear his throat as his stale body odor permeated the air.

"Hi, pretty lady." He grinned and grabbed my wrists.

His breath reeked like he'd eaten a dead rodent and rinsed his mouth with sour milk.

"Get your hands off of me," I howled as I tried to pull away. He gripped my forearms firmly and didn't budge an inch.

"I'm an attorney. I will take you down," I threatened more darkly. My body screamed with panic; my mind raced. Would this man try to kill me? Would he hurt me?

"Oh, a fancy lawyer, huh? Must mean you have more money on ya?"

Instinct took over, and I spat in his face. His eyes narrowed. He took his free hand and wiped the spit off his cheek. "I wasn't planning on hurtin' ya, but you may have changed my mind, bitch."

He cocked his arm back and raised his fist. I squeezed my eyes shut as I prepared for the inevitable blow I was about to endure.

But it never came.

I opened my eyes and saw the man's cocked fist frozen in mid-air. Another man behind him grabbed his arm and held it tightly.

"Let. Her. Go."

My attacker did as he was told, but only to face the other man squarely in the eye. My attacker snickered as he looked him up and down. "What are you going to do, huh?"

"This," the man said and punched my attacker in the solar plexus, which caused him to grasp at his chest and crumble to the ground.

I gasped, taking a heaping breath of fresh air. I didn't realize I'd been holding my breath until now.

I looked up and gazed into the eyes of the man who'd saved me.

It was William.

Chapter Twelve

WILLIAM

Amelia shuddered as her attacker scrambled to his feet and hobbled away.

"You saved me," she mumbled breathlessly.

Her casual appearance caught me off guard. I assumed the woman lived in a blazer. With her hair pulled back, her soft skin glowed under the streetlamp.

"It was nothing."

"How can I ever thank you?" she asked.

"No thanks needed." Last time she thanked me, a bastard restaurant manager shooed me away. Wasn't going through that again, not even for a hot meal.

"I mean it. Who knows what that creep would have done to me? Thank you so much."

"It's honestly not a big deal, lady."

Amelia threw her arms around my neck. I held my breath and pulled away. I didn't like people touching me, let alone hugging me. I wished she'd let go.

"It's freezing out here. Do you have someplace to go?"

"Don't worry about it," I said over my shoulder. I walked away, leaving her near the street behind me. It was my night for the shelter, and if I didn't go soon, they'd lock up, and I'd be locked out, stuck in the cold for another miserable night.

She jogged to catch up. "Hey! Wait up! There's gotta be something I can do for you?"

I paused and furrowed my brow.

"I mean it. Anything you want, it's yours," she promised.

Damn, this lady was persistent.

"I need to go. I have somewhere to be."

"How about a coffee? Then I can take you wherever you need to go?" Desperation lingered on her face.

I ran my fingers through my beard and pondered her offer. The shelter closed in forty-five minutes. And a coffee did sound nice. Maybe it'd warm me up?

"Fine."

Amelia smiled. "Know of any coffee shops around here?"

"I think there's an all-night cafe around the corner," I grumbled.

"Perfect!"

We walked in silence, and I noticed a large manila envelope poking out of her oversized purse. "What are you doing out here so late, anyway?"

Her cheeks reddened. "I needed a file from work."

"On a Friday night?"

"Yeah, I wanted to get a head start on some projects for work."

"You work a lot?"

"Way more than I should," she admitted.

"Don't you have a family?"

Amelia nodded. "I have a son, Charlie."

"No rich husband?"

"Divorced," she said flatly.

I studied her shadow upon the pavement and cleared my throat. "So, who watches your kid when you're working?"

"Well, he goes to school during the day, and then I have a

babysitter who usually picks him up after school and watches him until I get home."

"Poor kid."

Amelia paused. "What's that supposed to mean?"

I felt grateful for the dark ambiance as I blushed this time. "I only meant he probably misses you. It sounds like you work a lot."

"I try to set an example for him: if you work hard, you can take care of your family."

"Well, work hard enough, and you won't see your family."

I thought back to all the nights my mother put my dad's dinner in the microwave as he called to say he'd be late. He worked a lot, too, and I missed him all the time.

We approached the coffee shop, and I peered through the windows, noticing two groups of hipsters inside the cafe. My palms moistened, and my heart pounded. These were the kinds of kids who threw coins at me while I slept.

"I changed my mind. I don't want any coffee."

"What? Why?" Amelia asked, puzzled.

"I need to go. See you around."

She followed my gaze into the cafe and nodded. "How about I bring a couple of coffees and muffins out here?"

That might be okay, I thought.

"Sure. I guess."

She smiled and hurried inside to place the order. While I waited, I took refuge on a worn bench beside the cafe. It wasn't as nice as my bench, but it'd be okay for now. My stomach rumbled as I realized I'd forgotten what a muffin or a donut tasted like; it'd been years since I had one.

The bell on the door jingled, and Amelia stepped out of the cafe with two paper cups in tow and a bag stuffed to the brim. "Okay, I've got two blueberry muffins, two apple cinnamon pastries, and a double chocolate brownie."

"You trying to give me diabetes?"

Her face turned white as a ghost. "I'm sorry, I never thought—"

"I'm kidding," I interrupted. "Those all sound fine."

Her shoulders slackened as she handed me a coffee, the cup warming my hands at the first touch. I sipped the coffee in silence and closed my eyes to enjoy the liquid as it heated up my body a degree or two.

"So, tell me a little more about yourself," she asked.

"There's not much to tell," I replied, crumbs from the muffin pouring out of my mouth.

"How long have you been out here?" She hesitated before she finished the question.

"Six," I said.

"Years?" Her mouth dropped agape.

I nodded.

"Wow," was all she mustered.

"Have you tried to get a job?"

These were the types of questions I was all too familiar with living on the streets. People saw me and assumed I was lazy or addicted to crack. They couldn't be any further from the truth.

"I've tried, and I had a few."

"What happened? If you don't mind me asking."

While it seemed as though I was a participant on a 20 Questions game show, I sensed the genuine tone reflected within her inquiries.

"I've got some demons," I whispered.

She nodded politely. "I know all about those."

I raised an eyebrow and looked her up and down. "Yeah?"

"My father served. He never came home the same each tour."

"Yeah. War changes a person. So, tell me, why do you work so much? Especially if you've got a kid at home."

"Growing up, my father was tough on me. His work ethic was like nothing I'd ever seen before, even to this day. From a very young age, he instilled the same morals his parents taught him. I never wanted to disappoint him, so I worked my ass off in school," she explained.

"He proud of you now?"

"I'd like to think he would be," she trailed off.

At that moment, a part of my wall crumbled. Amelia lost her dad, too. With all of our differences, we finally shared one thing in common. Each of us lost a crucial puzzle piece to our soul. Neither of us could be whole again.

"I work hard to please him, even though he's not around. Pathetic, I know."

"What about your ex?" I asked, changing the subject.

She sighed. "He's about to get remarried to his soul mate."

"And how do you feel about that?"

"Well, our divorce was a good thing. It needed to happen for both our sanity, but it hurts to know he's moved on."

"Haven't you?"

"Parts of me have, but I think I'm still hung up on missing the idea of love rather than missing him in my life. I don't know if I'll ever fall in love again. You ever been in love?"

"Love is for the weak," I said.

The moon rested at the zenith of the night sky. The partying crowds continued to crawl and dominate the streets, and all our baked goods were gone.

"I should go now."

"Okay," Amelia said. "I'll order a Lyft. Where do you need to go?"

"Homeless shelter," I mumbled.

She didn't flinch, but instead typed away on her phone and nodded after a minute. "You know, I've been thinking of volunteering at the shelter?"

"Why?" I scoffed.

"My boss asked that I pick somewhere to volunteer. The attorneys are required to participate in the community."

"But why the homeless shelter?"

"Why not?"

"Don't you have better things to do with your time?" Sourness devoured my attitude.

"Sure, but then how would I have the opportunity to get to know you better?"

The Lyft car pulled up and honked its horn. Amelia smiled as she climbed into the car first. Deep down, a magnetic force drew me to her. Maybe she wasn't a stuck-up rich girl like I originally thought. Maybe I judged her too soon.

Chapter Thirteen

WILLIAM

I arrived at the Fort Benning Army Base in Georgia on a Sunday. The heat smacked me upside the head as soon as I stepped foot out of the airport. It was the first time I'd left New York City and the first time I'd be away from my mom for so long.

Last night, we had a quiet dinner with my uncle. My mom told me I could choose my "last meal," and I decided on pizza. I needed to savor the taste of city pizza while I could. I had no idea the next time I'd have city food, so I stuffed myself with as many slices as I could keep down. That ended up being about four slices at dinner and two for breakfast this morning. My uncle drove us to LaGuardia. The entire drive was silent as anticipation and sorrow filled the car. I wasn't sure if I'd be able to come home for a visit after basic training, so I knew it might be our last few minutes together for a very long time.

My uncle parked the car outside of Departures and helped me retrieve my bags from the trunk. My mom still hadn't spoken a word, but I couldn't blame her. She was about to "lose" her son a few years after she lost her husband. I think she had come to terms with my decision, though. While I could still see the sadness glowing in her emerald eyes, there was no anger or resentment.

My uncle slammed the trunk down, and we all looked at each other. I sighed heavily as my uncle pulled me into his arms.

"Be good, kid. Come home safely."

"Love you, Uncle Jim."

I choked back the tears as I approached my mom. She stood limply in a puffy winter coat which was now far too big for her weak body. He hair lay flat on her head, utterly devoid of life and luster. Guilt crushed my soul to leave her like this, but I knew Uncle Jim would take care of her.

"Well, this is it," I mumbled.

"I'm proud of you, son."

And, that's when I lost it. Sobs erupted deep within my belly, and I pulled her into my arms. I squeezed her, maybe too tightly, but I didn't care. I wanted this moment to last forever. I needed to remember I still had someone worth fighting for.

Uncle Jim checked his watch and tapped me on the shoulder. "Time to go."

I let go of my mom and nodded. I wiped away the tears, but couldn't fill the hole in my heart. I was leaving a piece of me behind. I was leaving New York behind, too.

My uncle and mom got back into the car, and I watched as they slowly drove away. With each passing second, my heart pounded harder and harder. The tough part was just beginning.

———

The first couple of days weren't too bad. Mostly because I only underwent administrative processes and filled out forms. The hardest part, at first, was getting my hair cut. Not that I had long hair or anything, but I had a few inches of curls most men and women envied. Hey, it's not my fault I caught people staring at my luscious locks during class!

I met my fellow trainees and even made a friend or two. Hudson was my age but twice as buff. I could tell he'd been training and preparing for months before enlisting. I found out he grew up in Manhattan only a few blocks away from me, too. Who could have guessed we'd spend our entire lives so close, only to meet hundreds of miles away in boot camp?

Then there was Spencer. Spence was a computer nerd who dreamt of becoming a famous war hero. I think he watched Saving Private Ryan one too many times, but he wouldn't admit that. He grew up in Brooklyn, but dropped out of NYU to enlist.

Hudson, Spencer and I became attached at the hip in no time. Not literally, but we were the only ones in our class from New York City. In a brand new world filled with strangers, at least we had a little semblance of home in each other. We chose bunks closest to each other and became best friends and roommates for the next several weeks.

Basic Training kicked my ass. The first time I met my drill sergeant, he woke us up in the middle of the night. He bellowed as he burst through the doors like the Hulk. He ordered us to drop and give him one hundred push-ups. After that he ordered us to run five miles. Whoever finished last had to run another five miles. I hadn't run since I was forced to in gym class back in high school, and even then we only had to run two miles at most. It didn't take long for sweat to cover my entire body and for me to believe I had developed asthma. Needless to say, I ran ten miles for the first time in my life that day. I thought I was in a nightmare or something. It turns out I went and joined the freaking military instead.

I immediately regretted my decision to enlist. What the hell was I thinking joining the military? I wasn't prepared for this. I wasn't made to run and hoist my sweaty body up from the ground. I was one more push-up away from quitting. My body ached, and I wanted it all to stop. I had no endurance. I wasn't a soldier. I was a spoiled rich kid who grew up affluent in New York City. Why did I ever think I was qualified to serve my country? The sergeants did their very best to break us down. I knew it was all part of the process, but it didn't matter. Basic was killing me inside.

Then, I remembered why I joined in the first place. My father's face appeared in my mind, and I thought back to the very last conversation we had. I told him I wasn't sure what I wanted to do with my life, that I felt lost, and I wasn't sure if college was right for me.

He looked straight into my eyes and told me, "Son, you can do whatever you set your mind to. Just don't set it to giving up. You'll find your place."

The next day he died. Did the universe plan it all? Was I meant to feel lost that night, only for him to tell me those final, wise words? Did he know someday I'd need the courage to keep going?

With that memory in mind, a jolt of lightning coursed through my veins. The adrenaline I desperately needed kicked in, and I managed to find the strength I needed to go on. I may have been miserable, but I didn't give up.

As training progressed, my body grew stronger and stronger. My endurance increased; my stamina exploded, and my mental stability evened out. The routine kept me focused, and the challenges kept me striving for success.

Hudson easily became the top of our Basic class, while Spence and I climbed the ranks every day. Soon, I didn't mind having someone telling me what to do and when to do it. Following orders simply became second nature to me, and I couldn't get enough of the structure and solid foundation forming underneath my feet. In retrospect, I'd begun to realize that it was necessary to break us down so the military could build us back up—only as soldiers, built to fight for our country.

I missed my mom and uncle more and more every day, however, the strength I'd found made it a lot easier to manage the distance between myself and my family. I called on Sunday nights if I could and talked to Mom for about five minutes or so. Uncle Jim filled me in as much as he could, but I knew there wasn't much to say. My mom's situation remained the same. She continued to grieve for my father and disappeared within herself. She was a ghost.

Graduation approached, and I prepared myself to slide into the next phase of my military career: Infantry Training.

Chapter Fourteen

AMELIA

A dull headache woke me up as a hangover greeted me with a vengeance. I squinted and wished I would have had the sense to shut the blinds before passing out. Even though I delighted in coffee and desserts last night, I ignored the voice in my head advising to have water and a Tylenol before falling asleep. The rays of sun shot through my window and shone directly into my eyes.

My phone rang, the ringtone echoing from my bedroom. I trotted to my room and wondered who could be calling me so early.

"Hello?" I squeaked.

"Mommy!"

"Oh, Charlie, I miss you so much already! How are you?"

Suddenly, my head throbbed a little less, and my heart grew fuller.

"I'm good, Mom. We're going to the zoo today!"

"Isn't it a little cold for that?"

"It's okay. I'm going to wear a coat."

"And gloves?" I reminded him.

He groaned. "Yes, I'll wear my gloves."

"I don't want you to get sick, sweetheart. That's all."

"You worry too much," Charlie said. Now, I groaned. A little more of Cal peeked through Charlie with every visit.

"Well, have a good day and call me later. Okay?"

"Bye, Mom!"

"I love you—"

He hung up. Oh, well. At least he called, right?

Part of me wished I had enough motivation to go to the gym and sweat out the rest of the toxins in my body. But I craved a greasy breakfast. First, though, I needed a shower more than anything.

I turned on the hot water as high as it would go. I prided myself on being tolerant of a scalding shower. In fact, I didn't feel clean without taking one with lava-temperature water. I lathered my body with my organic vanilla body wash, closed my eyes and breathed in the scent.

I hadn't told anyone, not that I had someone to tell, but I hadn't slept with anyone since Cal and I divorced. I know, I know. Crazy, right? But, I barely had enough time for Charlie and myself, let alone another man. Not to mention, being a single mom rarely affords an opportunity to go on dates or have relationships.

While some of my Cal-inflicted wounds were healed, I wondered if I was ready to get back out there and try dating again, if I ever scrounged up the time. It would be satisfying to have some more adult conversations outside of work. And someone to go out to dinner with. I loved venturing out with Charlie, but a girl needs more than pizza and chicken wraps for a meal. Charlie was still too young to try anything more sophisticated, so I settled on adapting to his diet instead.

I wanted a man to pick me up from my apartment, take me to a new restaurant where he ordered a snazzy bottle of wine, and let me choose any meal on the menu. To some, that might sound shallow, but I firmly believe in allowing others to spoil you if given a chance. I don't spoil myself often, so why not let another give it a try?

Thinking of men, I wondered where William was at this moment. Where did he go during the day? I decided I'd cruise around my office to see if I could spot him and ask him to join me for breakfast.

———

After several trips around the block, I was about to concede and go to breakfast by myself, but then I remembered dropping him off at the homeless shelter. Maybe he was still there?

I googled the address and drove over the shelter, which was located just outside the business district, bordering on the not-so-great part of town. Shattered glass littered the sidewalks, and several corner stores donned bars across their windows. I parked on the street right out front and made sure to lock my car.

I opened the shelter doors, and a foul stench greeted me. Inside, several volunteers chatted with the homeless men, women and children loitering around the giant hall with high, stretching ceilings. The place could use a few coats of paint and a good cleaning, but it was better than I expected. Across the room, accepting a hot cup of coffee in the line, stood William.

I strode over to him and cleared my throat to grab his attention.

"Hey!"

He looked over, glaring at me scathingly. "What are you doing here?"

"I was looking for you."

"Why?" His voice rattled with impatience.

"I thought I'd see if you wanted to catch breakfast or something. Charlie is with his dad for the next few weeks."

"Don't you have work to do or something?

Ouch.

"Well, uh, probably," I stuttered.

"I wish you wouldn't have come here," he said sourly.

"Why not?"

"You can't save me, Amelia. No one can."

My heart ached for the man before me. What happened in his life to cause him to feel like this?

"I'm not trying to save you or use you. I just want to spend some time with you."

"Find another charity case, okay?"

A man with graying hair and bifocal glasses walked over to us. "Hi, can I help you?"

"Yes, actually. My name is Amelia Montgomery. I was hoping to volunteer here. Do you have any openings?"

The man grinned a toothy smile. "We always need more volunteers! Right, William?"

William sneered and walked away.

"Don't worry about him," the man said. "He's always sort of broody."

"I can see that."

"Anyway, I'm Mark. Nice to meet you." He extended his hand. "Are you new to town?"

"Mhmm. I'm a new partner at the law firm down the street."

"Ross your boss?"

I nodded.

"Great man! Well, let me get you some paperwork, and we can get you all signed up."

William eyed me from across the room, and I couldn't help but wonder where his scathing stance came from. Last night, he seemed to open up a bit, but now he seemed as cold as ever.

Mark returned a few moments later with a few forms and an oversized t shirt with the shelter's logo plastered across the front. "Sorry, we only have extra-large left."

"I'm sure I'll manage." I smiled.

William watched me like a hawk while I filed out the

requested forms. I finished and handed them to Mark. "Great! When can you start?"

"How about now?" I suggested.

"Wonderful!" He clapped his hands. "We need to fold up all the cots and gather the linens to wash. Mind helping with that?"

"Not at all."

As requested, I folded the ruffled sheets across the thirty or so cots in the hall. I tried my best to stifle reactions to the soiled linens. Meanwhile, the rest of those in the shelter meandered out of the building somberly. It's too bad they couldn't stay, but I knew the building was used for other functions during the day.

William lingered by the exit as Mark thanked me again for my time. I promised I'd return once my scheduled allowed for it.

"Feel better?" William asked quietly as he leaned against the wall.

"What do you mean?" I narrowed my eyes.

"Now that you've helped the homeless and poor?" William said with a snarky tone. He crossed his arms across his body.

"Did I do something or say something to offend you last night?" I asked. I thought back to our time together the previous night. I thought we had a good time. Well, as good a time as a homeless man and a single mother can have while sipping coffee out in the cold.

"No, why?"

"You're awfully salty today. I'm just trying to help, you know?" I shrugged.

William turned his back and opened the shelter doors. "Yeah, I know. Sorry," he said over his shoulder. His face softened, then, just before he walked outside and let the door slam behind him.

After volunteering, I couldn't bring myself to head back home. I drove to the waterfront a few blocks away and breathed a sigh of relief that I'd worn sneakers and a warm hoodie this morning. Seagulls filled the sky as the sun peeked through the clouds. The water reflected the sunlight and sparkled brilliantly. Families, couples, and singles roamed the path along the water. I'd have to bring Charlie here when he came home. He'd love to fly his kite here.

While I strolled along the smooth asphalt path, I spotted an elderly couple sitting on a bench, gazing at the water and holding hands. Would I ever have a love like that? Would I ever love again? Would I ever slow down working so much to even give myself the chance? I thought back to just a few days ago when I forgot to pick up Charlie from school because I was so involved with my research. What else was I sacrificing by slaving away at my desk?

The couple sat silently together; they didn't need to talk to enjoy each other's company. Isn't that the best kind of love? The love so rooted in your soul that just being in each other's presence is enough?

My heart ached with desire. The desire to be wanted. The desire to be cherished. The desire to never be taken for granted. However, I knew deep down, right now I didn't have the time to find someone who could provide all of these things. Time, there's never enough of it, is there?

I thought maybe I had a better chance of winning the lottery than ever falling in love again.

Chapter Fifteen

AMELIA

The following week dragged as though time decided to move backward instead of forward. I missed Charlie more than my soul could bear. My workload increased tenfold, and William either relocated or hid from me.

I couldn't remember a time I felt more alone. I fell asleep in silence and woke up to silence. I ate lunch by myself and ordered take out every night. I couldn't believe I agreed to let Charlie go with his father for two whole weeks. If the first week was this heartbreaking, I knew the second week would only be worse.

On Monday morning, I arrived to work twenty minutes late for a client meeting. It was the Monday-est Monday ever. There was an accident on the highway which took up two of the three lanes. The car ahead of me slammed on their brakes out of nowhere, which then led me to brake in a panic. Of course, I was holding my Starbucks double latte at the time, and it spilled all over me. What the hell was it with me and spilling hot beverages on myself?

Then, someone parked in my designated spot in the parking lot. As much as I wanted to park behind them, blocking them in,

I decided to take the high road and find another spot, which happened to be three more blocks away from my office.

Oh, and it didn't stop there. Of course not! While I jogged to the office, my heel caught in a sidewalk crack and broke cleanly off. I hadn't brought a second pair of shoes with me.

I struggled to hold back my tears. Did I do something wrong recently? Was karma coming back to kick me in the ass for something I did in a past life? Maybe this was punishment for staying up until three in the morning working on a case? My body rebelled against me.

I hobbled into the office and caught a few sympathetic glares from female employees and haughty stares from my male co-workers. I knew I still needed to prove my worth to some people here. It was survival of the fittest in a law firm, and at this exact moment, I wasn't all that fit.

When I approached the building's elevators, fate bitch-slapped me again: all three cars were out of order. I checked my watch and saw I was now thirty minutes late for my meeting. I burst out laughing to the point I couldn't breathe. People all around me gawked with confusion. Alas, I had to make the painful decision to climb four flights of stairs in a broken pump. After the first flight, my ankle screamed in agony from the imbalance of having two different shoe heights. Then, I yelled, "Fuck it!" and took off both shoes so I could jog the rest of the way to my office.

I reached my floor and dashed past my secretary, then stormed into the conference room ready and willing to beg on my knees for forgiveness from my client. However, once I entered the designated conference room, I realized it was empty.

Shit! Did they leave?

I ran back out to my secretary's desk. "Karen, did Mr. Franko leave already?"

She looked puzzled. "I'm not sure I know what you're talking about?"

"My meeting today," I gasped. "I know I'm late. Did he leave?"

Karen covered her mouth as she giggled. "Uh, Amelia, I'm sorry, but that meeting is next week."

My proverbial ceiling shattered as relief and joy flooded my soul. While I was angry with myself for mixing up the dates, I couldn't be happier with my mistake. I had another chance to make my meeting on time and not make a fool out of myself. But, that meant I still had to manage the rest of the day with a broken heel, a stained outfit and probably a permanent feeling of being out of breath. If only I'd put myself to bed and didn't work myself to exhaustion last night!

"Thanks, Karen!" I said slowly.

"Rough morning?"

"You have no idea!"

"Can I get you anything?"

"Yeah, a new blouse and size eight heels, please."

"Coming right up," Karen said. She rummaged under her desk and pulled out a pair of black suede pumps and a simple black button-up top.

"Are you serious right now?"

"I always keep a few extra things here, just in case of emergency." She smiled.

"Oh my God! You're amazing! My angel!" I reached over her desk and hugged her. A few knick-knacks toppled over during our embrace, which I apologized for.

"Can I get you some coffee?"

"Yes, please! I seem to be wearing the one I purchased this morning."

While Karen happily went to collect a fresh cup of coffee for me, I went into my office, leaned back in my chair and closed my eyes.

What a morning!

Karen popped into my office carrying a mug filled to the brim with steaming, hot coffee.

"You are a lifesaver," I said gratefully.

"Just here to help!" Karen chirped.

Karen was in her late-fifties and acted like my second mother. I'd only been at the new firm for a few weeks, and she made me quite comfortable the instant I met her. She was beyond helpful and always on top of her game. She could read my mind and know exactly what I needed from her without asking. Now, she was not only my work-mom, but she was also my fairy godmother, too!

"You know, Amelia—may I call you Amelia?"

"Of course!"

"It may not be my place, but from what I can tell, you may be putting too much stress on yourself. You seem exhausted!"

I rubbed my eyes and exhaled. "Yeah, I may need to slow down a bit."

"Life here is a marathon, not a sprint." She winked.

"Thanks, Karen. I'll try to remember that!"

"Oh, and one more thing," Karen said. "Hector quit, so until they find a new janitor, we will have to all chip in and tidy up around here."

"Oh, I'm sorry to hear that! I liked Hector."

"His wife had a baby, and he decided to quit to become a stay-at-home dad!"

"Good for him. Not good for us." I smiled.

"So, if you know of anyone looking for a job, you should ask them to apply."

I nodded, and Karen stepped out of my office to return to her desk.

I thought of William. Surely he'd be interested in the job, right? Any job had to be better than no job? I remember he mentioned having demons, but maybe he'd exorcised them since his last attempt at earning a paycheck? I tucked the new piece of information away for when I could find William and let him know about the position.

I sipped the coffee Karen brought me, snickering once I read
the message painted on the mug, "Keep Calm and Slow Down."

The rest of the morning sped by as I worked on three matters,
met with Ross about one of them and walked my paralegal
through what I needed her to work on for me. By lunchtime, my
stomach rumbled. I'd accidentally skipped breakfast except for
my cup and a half of coffee. I took the elevator, which had conve-
niently been restored after I arrived at work, down to the cafeteria. I thought about ordering two entrees to satisfy my hunger,
but knew I should only have one lunch, because I couldn't afford
any more outfits for work. The pizza on display called to me, but
I chose baked chicken and veggies instead. Not to mention, I
ordered pizza three times since Charlie was gone. I feared I might
turn into a slice if I ate one more piece!

I scarfed almost my entire lunch, and then, out of the corner
of my eye, I saw William walk by outside. I did a double take
because I wasn't sure if it was him at first, but it was; I could feel
it. I stood so quickly, my chair fell backward, but I ignored the
stares, once again, and strode toward the stairs which led to the
street outside. As soon as the cool air touched my face, I took off
my borrowed heels so as not to repeat what happened this morning. The chilled sidewalk burned my feet, but they'd warm up
eventually.

I saw William turn the corner a block ahead of me, so I
revived my inner track star and raced after him. He could hide
from me, but he couldn't run! It took a minute or two, but I
finally caught up with him. I reached for his arm, but he turned
around before I could touch him.

"Why are you following me?"

"William," I gasped. "I—need—to—talk—to you."

He rolled his eyes. "About what?"

"Can we go somewhere to talk? It's kind of cold out here." I
shivered in my stockings while I continued to hold my heels in
my hands.

"We can talk right here."

"Okay, well, I wanted to tell you that my firm has a job opening, and I think it would be perfect for you!"

He eyed me suspiciously. "What kind of job?"

"It's for maintenance and cleaning." I shuffled my feet. "Do you think you may want to apply?"

He snorted. "Sure, let me grab a clean copy of my resume, my freshly laundered suit, and I'll be there in a jiffy. And, being a lawyer, you should know I can't get a job without a permanent address."

Damn, I forgot about that part.

"I know your situation isn't ideal—"

"Ideal? Do you realize I'm homeless? My life isn't ideal, or less than ideal; it's a fucking nightmare." He stalked away before I could reply.

"What are you afraid of?" I called out.

He stopped and whipped around. "Afraid? I'm not afraid of anything."

"Then why won't you give it a shot, huh? What do you have to lose if you already have nothing?"

He bit his lip and thought for a moment. "Look at me, Amelia. How could I ever walk into a job interview looking like this, even if I found someplace to sleep that wasn't a public bench?"

Now it was my turn to ponder the situation. I thought back to how I accidentally packed one of Cal's suits before I left Candlebrook. He left it in the closet in the dry cleaning wrapping, and I assumed it was one of mine when I packed. The plastic covering the suit was nearly opaque, and so it went along for the ride when I moved.

"I have a suit you could borrow. I'm not sure it will be a perfect fit, but it should work well enough."

Despite William's lack of a consistent diet, he was still about the same size as Cal.

"Hmm, okay. Well, what about this?" He shook his shaggy chestnut hair and pointed to his unkempt beard.

"I've never told you this before, William, but I'm one hell of a living room barber. I cut Charlie's hair like a champ!"

"Fine," he said.

"Really? You'll give it a shot?"

"I'll try."

"Operation Makeover is just beginning!"

William stared inquisitively.

"You know, because you were in the military? Operation Makeover?" I couldn't help but laugh at myself.

"I get it," he said. "I just don't think it's funny."

Despite his sour demeanor, I was ready to help William get out of his street clothes and into a suit. A rare feeling overwhelmed me then: what would William look like in a suit? What would he look like after a cut and shave? I'd find out soon enough.

Chapter Sixteen

AMELIA

William's interview was scheduled for Friday morning at nine AM. On Thursday, much to his dismay, William met me by my car, and I drove us back to my apartment. We'd grown close enough by now, I felt safe bringing him to my home. Plus, Charlie was still with his father.

I'm not exactly sure where he thought we were going to go, but he glared loathingly out of the car window during the ride to my humble abode. I knew it must be hard for him to see someone else live in luxury, but I genuinely wasn't trying to rub it in his face. If anything, I wanted him to have the same kind of life in the very near future. I know maintenance wouldn't pay as much as my salary, but it was a start.

My doorman smiled as we walked into the foyer and I wished him a good evening. Despite his jovial greeting, I caught him staring at William with narrowed eyes. I ignored it and hoped William didn't see it, but I'm sure he did. He noticed everything. He could tell just by the look on my face if I was having a good day or a bad day. He knew if I had something I wanted to say or if I merely wanted to co-exist in silence. It was almost weird how observant he was. I hadn't known anyone who could pick up on my non-verbal signals so well. Not even Cal when we were married.

"So, are you ready for a new look?" I asked as I found the Superman cape I used when I cut Charlie's hair.

"Just don't butcher it, okay?" Hesitation and possibly regret bloomed within his demeanor.

"I would never!" I said, aghast as I clutched at my chest. I couldn't believe this tough warrior was wearing a comic book hero cape and about to let me chop off his scraggly street hair.

"Ready?"

"As I'll ever be, Montgomery."

I took a deep breath and cut the first lock of William's hair. It dropped to the floor, and his eyes followed its descent.

"Not so bad, huh?"

"That was only the first cut," he said. "There's still time for you to mess it up."

"You better watch your tone, or else I'll give you a mullet."

"I wouldn't doubt it."

"I heard that!"

For the next half hour, I meticulously cut William's hair and prayed to God I wouldn't mess it up. It was probably his first haircut in years; I didn't want to disappoint him. Especially considering he didn't appear to have high expectations of my skills. I cut the long pieces and started trimming and styling the rest. My stereo played The Lumineers, the heavenly sound echoing throughout the apartment. I'd lit a few Yankee candles too. I wanted William to feel at ease and hoped the cupcake scented one would help.

"Ready to see your new look?"

"You mean my hack job?"

"I'm still holding the scissors," I warned.

When he didn't respond, I held up the mirror and watched as his eyes focused in on his reflection with fierce concentration.

"Whoa!"

That was all the reassurance I needed to hear.

"I bought a new razor and some shaving cream for you, too. It's in the bathroom."

William nodded and took off the Superman cape. He strode to the bathroom with a noticeable spring in his step. I poured myself a glass of wine and patted myself on the shoulder. Now, I just had to sweep up the hair and wait for him to shave.

Twenty minutes passed, and silence filled the apartment. I knocked on the door. "Everything okay in there?"

"Yeah!" he called back.

"Well, what's taking so long, then? Let me see what you look like."

My heart thudded with excitement. I felt like I was living *Jumanji* when Robin Williams comes out of the game looking like a wild man, only to clean himself up afterward and become a brand-new man.

The door opened slowly, and I stepped back to give William room to come out. My palms were sweating as I held my breath. He inched out of the room with his head down. I couldn't see his face.

"Well?"

Then, he looked up, and my breath caught in my throat. The man who stood before me looked like an entirely new person. If I hadn't known any better, I would have thought William jumped out of the window, and a distant cousin took his place in my bathroom.

"Wow," was all I could muster.

A warming sensation maneuvered its way to my loins while my pulse raced. William was... HOT. His haircut made him look not only like a new man, but a professional one. He shaved his beard but kept a five o'clock shadow, which made me imagine the sensation of his scruff against my cheek. I wondered how his lips would taste. Wait! Whoa! What was happening to me? I only met this guy a few weeks ago, and I was imagining all this? I scolded myself and put down my wine.

His eyes pierced my soul, and it felt as though I was meeting William for the very first time. I imagined all the girls who must have chased after him years ago.

"That a good wow or a bad wow?"

"Good," I gulped.

He blushed, and adrenaline pumped through my veins. My body hadn't reacted this way to a man in a very long time. This was dangerous. Very freaking dangerous.

"How do you feel?"

"Like I lost a few pounds in hair," he said with a smile.

"You look, um-"

"What?" His hands darted to his face.

"Handsome," I finally managed to say.

He exhaled. "Thanks. And, thank you for helping me with, you know, everything." It was the first time he sounded more grateful than bitter.

"Thank you for letting me."

My hormones and wine had gone straight to my head. I hoped I wouldn't scare William away. Especially because we'd come so far from the first time we met. He opened up to me a little more each time we were together and lowered his walls a touch by letting me cut his hair.

Yesterday, I took a last-minute volunteering shift at the shelter. When I arrived, the other volunteers, ranging in ages from sixteen to sixty, prepared dinner to serve to those in attendance. Mark handed me an apron and a hairnet. William's eyes nearly bulged out of his head when I served him his portion of meatloaf and mashed potatoes.

"You again?" he asked.

"Me again," I confirmed.

After dinner, we took a walk around the block. A cot was already reserved for him, so he didn't have to worry about someone stealing his place for the night. We strolled the streets and gazed at the stars overhead. Even though the city lights washed out most of the stars, a few constellations peeked through.

"My dad died on September eleventh," he'd said.

My heart lurched. "I'm so sorry to hear that."

"That's why I enlisted after college. I wanted to fight for his honor."

"That's a very honorable reason."

"Are you scared you'll miss out on Charlie's life?" he had asked me.

"What do you mean?"

"Well, by working so much. Aren't you afraid you'll miss something?"

I considered what William asked. Of course I wanted to be in Charlie's life as much as possible, he was my only child, I loved him more than anyone could love another human being. I wanted to see him grow and live to his fullest potential. I wanted to be there to kiss his bruises, wipe away his tears after his first heart break and watch him walk across the stage at graduation. I often imagined the day I'd dance with him at his wedding or hold my grandchild for the first time. Would I actually miss out if I kept up my current pace at work? Cal constantly warned me when we were together that I'd turn into a ghost of a mother. I'd be in Charlie's life, but only as a fleeting image of who I once was or could have been.

"I try to be there for him as much as I can. I can only do so much being a single mom."

"We can always do better," he had said thoughtfully.

A crater appeared in my gut. Could I do better? Could I be home more for Charlie? I shook away the revelry and brought myself back to the present moment.

"So," he said.

"So?"

"What now?"

"You gotta try on the suit!" I reminded him.

William shuffled his feet. "That's right. Uh, but is a suit really necessary? I mean, it's only a maintenance job."

"I don't think it could hurt your chances. Better to overdress than underdress, right?"

"Uh, yeah. Right."

I dashed to my bedroom, and William followed. I opened my walk-in closet with him at my heels, then handed him the suit from the clothing rack by my shoes.

"This closet looks like something out of a movie." His eyes bulged and he ran his hands along the clothing neatly hung with care.

"Well, Cal never let me have anything like this at our house, so I figured I'd splurge this time around."

William looked down at the suit I'd handed him. "So, this is your ex's suit, then?"

"Yes, but it should fit fine. Go! Try it on." I ushered him back into the bathroom.

"Do you mind if I take a quick shower first? I don't want to get the suit all dirty." He shrugged as color returned to his cheeks again.

I never spent much time thinking about how William managed to bathe, if he did at all. By now, I'd grown accustomed to his musk.

"Not at all. Be my guest."

He smiled and closed the bathroom door behind him. He turned the water on, and the powerful jets pounded against the tiles. While William showered, I stood by the island in the kitchen and started dinner.

I didn't have too many ingredients available to make something super fancy and filling, but I had everything I needed to make fettuccine alfredo. I mixed the ingredients for the sauce on the stovetop when I heard the bathroom door click open followed by soft footsteps sounding on the hardwood floor.

I looked up, and my heart stopped: William decked out in a suit combined with his new haircut shocked me like an electric current.

"Does it fit okay?" He slowly turned around.

"It's perfect!" I exclaimed. "You're going to wow everyone tomorrow. I just know it."

"I'm not getting my hopes up," he said.

"What are you talking about? You're going to knock 'em dead!"

"I don't have much job experience outside of the military, Amelia." Frown lines creased his handsome face. "And it's not like I can use my old bosses as references for the jobs I had after I left the Army. Plus, you're still forgetting I don't have a permanent address."

"You deserve a second chance, okay?"

He stared at his feet, and I sensed his walls build back up again.

I cleared my throat. "Listen, William. It's a great opportunity, and we've all gotta start somewhere. I put in a good word for you, and even though I'm new myself, I seem to have some pull already."

He nodded. "Well, what if I get it?"

"Then we celebrate!"

"I mean, what would I do for an alarm clock to get there on time? What would I do for transportation?" I saw the panic in his eyes as his chest rose and fell quickly. He struggled to catch his breath and sat down on the living room couch.

I lowered the heat on the alfredo sauce and strode over to him. I wrapped my arms around his neck and squeezed him against my body. It was the first time he let me give him a hug. His acceptance of my gesture surprised me, but I rolled with it.

"Everything will be okay. I promise. I will help you with anything you need."

William finally pulled away, but his smile lingered. In that instant, everything made sense: we were magnets, finally connected, fitting perfectly in each other's arms.

"And, I *do* have a solution for your address problem."

"What do you mean?" His smile wavered.

"I was talking to Mark, and he told me about a halfway house near the shelter."

"That place costs money," William said.

"Well, it's a good thing I have some of that."

"I can't let you do that." He shook his head, a frown forming on his face.

"Don't worry. You can pay me back once you get the job." I waited for the smile he wore earlier to return.

"I can't accept your money.

"What if I charge you interest? Like a loan?"

"I'll have to think about it," he answered, biting his lip.

As much as I tried to help him, it felt like taking two steps forward and three steps back. I realized he wasn't used to this much help, having lived on the streets for the past six years, but it was time he figured it out.

I heard how dry and hot the desert was, but it didn't set in just how brutal the conditions were until I traveled to Afghanistan for my first tour overseas. The heat suffocated me, and I felt as though I was breathing in the sand with every breath. The first day, I sweated through my uniform within the first hour and reminded myself to drink as much water as possible to avoid dehydration. Even with the air conditioning turned on in our makeshift tin shelters, the temperature still read eighty degrees.

The desert went on for miles and miles, far past my eye could see. I never thought I'd miss the sight of grass and trees, but I did. Luckily, I had Spence and Hudson by my side. We endured together, as always. I never imagined the camaraderie we shared was possible. We relied on each other more than anyone else and entrusted our lives to each other's protection.

We didn't know a whole heck of a lot about our first mission when we landed, but it soon became clear what it entailed. There was a group of Taliban rebels taking down soldiers delivering emergency supplies on the ground to other military bases, and civilians caught in the middle suffered fatal consequences.

Three humvees in the past month alone were attacked as they planned to deliver food, medicine, and clean water. Our goal was to hunt those motherfuckers down and show them not to fuck with America.

First, we needed intel of who these bastards were, where they were coming from, and the kind of weaponry they carried. With the help of several intelligence agencies, we found out the specific Taliban group consisted of twenty to twenty-five men from a local village. They had automatic weapons and kept a post of men who rotated shifts as they held a lookout for American planes, helicopters, and foot soldiers.

We had a few locals on our side, but the majority of those in the area were Taliban. Once the few and far between Arab men joined our side, we had to provide them protection. If their village or the Taliban ever found out they teamed up with the Americans, they and their families would be slaughtered without question. We had trouble communicating with them at first, as their English was broken. But with the help of an interpreter, working together became easier and easier every day.

Sama, the interpreter, grew up in a village not too far away. She was a badass who intimidated most of the men on base. She helped ease the tensions many times, too. When you bring two cultures together, there's bound to be a few disagreements. It also didn't help that some of the men referred to the Iraqi soldiers as "camel fuckers." As I said, it wasn't easy at first. While the days and weeks passed, though, we taught each other bits and pieces of our own cultures. Soon, the Iraqis on our side became obsessed with American movies, and we became enthralled with the local cuisine. I'd never had hummus before, but once I tasted it, I couldn't get enough.

During a morning briefing, our captain told us we were about to see some serious action. The plan was simple: a decoy plane, flown and controlled offsite, would distract the Taliban group we sought so a humvee could get through to bring the emergency supplies the local civilian villages desperately needed. Most supplies traveled through the Pakistan border. Unfortunately, we couldn't always trust those at the border not to tip off members of the Taliban. While the decoy plane drew out the terrorists, we'd hone in on them and take down as many of those fuckers as we could.

We spent the rest of the day relaxing, as we knew our orders didn't begin until the following morning. Many of us liked to kick a soccer ball around to waste time. Others sat in a circle and played hand after hand of blackjack and poker. If we weren't working out, telling stories, or playing games, we didn't have much else to occupy our time while we awaited orders. Spence, Hudson and I watched as the others sweated like pigs kicking the damn ball back and forth to each other. We'd just finished working out and now relaxed under the brutal sun. Even though our thermometer said it was well over one hundred degrees, we couldn't stand the idea of going to lie down in our cots. We already slept as much as we could; I was getting bored of sleeping. Sixteen year old me would be disappointed.

"Can you believe we're here?" Spence asked.

"I can't, man. Feels surreal," Hudson replied.

"Whatever happens, I'm happy to have you guys by my side."

"Oh, look! William's getting soft on us!" Hudson said as Spence chuckled.

"I may be an only child, but you two fuckers are my brothers."

"Who knew we'd be here together?" Spence asked.

"The big man upstairs did," Hudson said. "He brought us together, and he'll keep us together."

We passed around a big jug of room temperature water and reminisced about training and all the hard work we'd put in to get here. It felt like the last supper, but I hoped we'd all make it out alive. I couldn't lose anyone else in my life; I really couldn't. Burying my dad was hard enough; I couldn't say goodbye to my brothers, too. I thought about what Hudson said about God bringing us together. While I was a man of country, I wasn't a man of church. But the more I thought about it, the more I wondered what the chances were of us being brought together, of us serving together. Maybe it was God, or perhaps it was fate. Either way, I knew if I had to be in the hot-ass desert, I was happy to be here with Spence and Hudson.

Adrenaline coursed through my veins that night. I couldn't sleep. None of us could. I heard my brothers toss and run on their cots for hours on end. This was it: what we'd trained for. This was why we were here. This was my chance to honor my father's memory and remove as much evil from the world as I possibly could. Did it bother me I wielded power to take someone's life? Not in the least bit, because I knew when they flew into the World Trade Center, killing hundreds and hundreds of people, they believed in their cause. And I believed in mine. For my country and my father, I would delight in killing as many terrorists as possible.

At oh-six-hundred, a knock pounded on our shelter as the Captain came in and said two simple yet captivating words, "Let's go."

We suited up. Hudson and Spence each sported a giddy grin to match mine. Everything we'd learned, everything we stood for, would be tested today. We packed the rest of our gear, most of which had already been put together in each of our multiple packs. I checked to make sure I had my bulletproof vest, ammo pouches, medical kit, grenades, canteen, ear plugs, night vision goggles, sunglasses, gloves, wet weather gear, helmet, and my M-4 rifle I'd named Sally. Don't ask me why.

To civilians, it would seem nearly impossible to carry the weight into battle, but for me, it was like any other day. We'd walked miles and miles with our gear in training to prepare us. I was ready. Although, I felt like I'd traveled into the pages of Tim O'Brien's masterpiece.

The decoy plane was set to land about twenty miles south of our base. My battalion would drive to the planned location in our military-grade convoys to meet the Taliban once they arrived to shoot the plane. Electricity in the air surged through my veins as we drove to Location X. A few men's faces glowed a bright shade of green, but the majority of us wore smirks of revenge across our faces. In a pocket, I carried a photograph of my dad. As the Captain announced we were less than five miles away, I pulled out the picture and stared intently into my father's eyes. I missed him like hell, and I still felt as though a piece of my soul was ripped away that day. I carried the burden of grief everywhere I went. But I'd never forgotten how much I loved my father and how much he loved me. It was this love that helped me carry on. My love for my father would help me through this.

The convoys stopped, and we all lurched forward. Our Captain reported to us through our earpieces and ordered us to go outside and fall into position. In a half hour, the decoy plane would arrive and draw out the Taliban forces just in time for us to surprise them and ruin their day.

When we emptied the convoy, my battalion picked ideal divets in the earth to post up and wait for the rat fuckers to come out of hiding. That was the hardest part: waiting for time to pass. My heart pounded forcibly against my chest, and nervousness coursed through my veins. Sweat soaked my body already, despite darkness blanketing the sky. During the night, Afghanistan dropped well below comfortable temperatures. Sometimes, the relief was much-needed, and others, I froze my ass off.

We still had about twenty minutes until we expected to see the Taliban. The stillness in the air calmed me for a little while, but I knew we were only in the eye of the storm. In fact, the quiet morphed into an intensity we all simultaneously felt. I imagined all the scenes of every war movie I ever watched. None of them prepared me for this moment, though. Soon, I'd face life or death. Soon, everything would change.

"You ready for this?" I asked Spence and Huddy, a nickname he despised, but I used it all the same.

They both nodded and smiled broadly. "Let's get 'er done, bro," Hudson said.

"Time to kill some terrorist fucks!" Spence agreed.

Then, shots rang out. My brothers and I looked around to the source of the gunfire.

"It's an ambush!" Our Captain called out. "Come back to the convoys now!"

While most people would fall into hysteria, calm washed over me. I knew what I had to do, even if all hell had broken loose. Spence, Hudson and I had each other's backs as we rose and shot several bullets toward the fighters encroaching our group.

"Fuck you!" Spence yelled.

Somehow, the Taliban knew we'd be here. They tried to kill us, as they killed so many Americans before us.

Spence, Hudson and I made our way back to the convoy. Spence, a couple of paces ahead of us, led the way. A handful of seconds passed, and then an explosion erupted around us all. I saw Spence fly through the air like a toy, and shock rippled through my body. A motherfucking IED. Then, it all went black.

That night, William slept on the couch so we could ride together to the office in the morning. We'd accidentally gotten a little too tipsy after dinner, so I set my alarm an hour earlier than normal so we could work on his resume together. Usually, I'm much more responsible when it comes to drinking on a work night, but something about William had me letting my guard down.

I softly tapped William's shoulder to wake him up. After a minute, he hadn't moved a muscle so I shook him more abruptly.

"Wake up, sleepy head!" I sang brightly.

William tensed up as soon as he opened his eyes, and the anxiety in the air felt palpable. He jumped up, grabbed at his belt and pulled out a pocket knife.

"Whoa!"

He looked around with a gaze of fright upon his face. I recognized that face, though; it was the same one my father wore when he awoke from one of his night terrors. He, too, suffered the consequences of combat. I was no stranger to this look. After a moment, William mumbled an apology and put the knife away.

I pulled a chair over to the couch and held my MacBook in my lap. The aroma of coffee wafted through the air, and William eyed me as I pulled my robe tighter across my chest. I realized too late I wasn't wearing a bra.

Once he sat up on the couch, I pulled up the resume template I downloaded from the internet. Formatting his resume didn't take as long as I expected considering he hadn't held a steady job after being released from the military. But, I beefed it up as much as I could to make it look impressive.

"Do you think that sounds too cocky?" William asked as he pointed to the line I'd just written.

"Not at all. Nothing wrong with showing off your accomplishments," I replied eagerly.

"Wait, I think there's a typo." William reached for the laptop and his hand brushed against mine. "Oh, sorry." He pulled back as though he touched a hot stove, but the feeling of his skin against mine sent a shock wave through my body.

"Fixed it." Our eyes locked and fire burned between our gaze.

I wanted another excuse to feel his touch, but it was time to get ready for work.

"You're going to do fine!" I promised for the one-hundredth time. "The maintenance manager is really friendly."

William nodded and swallowed. He hid in the bathroom after we finalized his resume. I needed to get in there myself, but I didn't want to rush him or bother him while he got ready. His day was much more important than mine. I wasn't meeting with any clients today, so I used Charlie's bathroom instead.

I didn't have very much makeup in my bedroom to use in our second bathroom, but I had just enough to cover up the pesky bags underneath my eyes and apply a coat of mascara to my lashes. While I dug in my nightstand drawer, I also found a faint pomegranate lipstick to wear. I glanced at my watch and realized if we didn't leave soon, we'd both be late.

"William, are you almost ready? We gotta go, like now."

"Coming!" He opened the bathroom door, and the suit looked just as dashing on him as it did last night. The only difference was William's face appeared quite a bit more green than before.

I handed him a banana and a to-go cup of coffee.

"You're going to knock 'em dead, soldier!" I punched him in the arm, and he looked as though he wanted to puke on my shoes. I wanted to punch *myself* after that. Why did I do that?

We passed the guard in the foyer, and I couldn't help but smile as he did a double take at William. I'd brought a shaggy homeless man home, only to leave the next day with a debonair hunk crushing it in his Giorgio Armani suit.

William sat in the passenger seat, and I noticed his hands shook while they held his resume and cup of coffee. I'd run out of motivational tidbits, which was probably for the best. So, we rode to the office in silence. He slurped his coffee now and again, but I'm sure the caffeine only increased his nerves. We parked in my spot, which hadn't been taken today, and walked in silence to my firm's building. When we passed William's bench, I noticed him glance at it out of the corner of my eye.

William held the door open for me as we entered the building. I signed him in at the front desk and pulled him into my arms. I didn't care if anyone witnessed our embrace. When I was around William, I only thought about him. Screw the people around us.

"You're going to do great, okay? Just remember what we practiced. Oh, and have the receptionist call me when you're finished. I want to hear all about it!"

"Thanks, Amelia."

I left William in the foyer as he waited for our maintenance manager to bring him into the conference room for his interview. I wished I could go with him, but I had to let him go for the time being.

In my office, I spent the next hour chewing on my pen and glancing at the clock. For the life of me, I couldn't understand what was taking so long. The interview should have lasted about a half hour, tops. I checked our office messenger and saw Andy, the maintenance manager, was still in "Meeting" mode.

To distract myself, I poured another cup of coffee and rechecked my emails.

"Everything okay?" Karen peeked her head into my office.

"Uh, I think so."

"That doesn't sound so convincing. What's up?"

"Come in," I said, ushering her inside. "So, I met someone."

Her face lit up like a Christmas tree. "You did?!"

"Oh, not like that!" I corrected. "William is just a friend, but he's interviewing for the open maintenance job."

Karen eyed me. "Just a friend? Is this the same William you've mentioned before?"

Karen was probably the only friend I'd made since moving here. She acted so motherly toward me, it felt as though I actually had a mom in my life again. I'm sure my own mother approved from the big puffy clouds upstairs. I'm sure she was happy I had someone in my life to lean on. It's not like I could give my ex mother-in-law a call to talk about men, right? Even though everyone at my firm was friendly, I sometimes had a hard time opening up to new people, except for Karen.

"Yes, the same one."

"I thought I saw a handsome new face downstairs when I came in this morning." She grinned. "He's very cute. You sure you're just friends?"

As I was about to shoo her away, my phone rang, and I jumped in my seat. The caller ID read "Reception," and I stood as I picked the receiver up from the cradle.

"Yes?"

"William asked that I call you and let you know he's waiting for you downstairs."

"Thanks, Beth!"

"Your knight in shining armor awaits," Karen teased.

I stuck my tongue out and raced to the elevators. Karen had a way of bringing out the kid in me sometimes.

"Well, how did it go?" I asked William as we sat down at a corner table in the cafeteria.

He looked crestfallen, and my heart broke. Then his frown disappeared, and a sly smile spread across his freshly shaven cheeks.

"I got it," he said.

I gasped. "You did? I knew you would!" Heads turned at my sudden outburst, but I ignored them. "I'm so happy for you! Did you tell them you'd have a permanent address soon?"

"Yeah, they said it was no problem. I just have to show proof of the address after I move in."

I hugged him for the second time that morning and breathed in his fresh, mouthwatering scent.

"I start on Monday."

"That's great!"

"So, there's something I wanted to talk to you about," he said, his smile fading.

"Anything."

"I was wondering if I could borrow a little money." He swallowed. "I promise I'll pay you back with interest, but I need a little something until I get my first paycheck. You know, for some new clothes and stuff."

I knew this must be difficult to ask for, but I had no problem helping him. "Of course, whatever you need.

"Really?" I saw a bead of sweat roll down his face.

"Yeah, of course. I could use a shopping trip myself.

"I think I'm going to go take a walk to get some fresh air," he said.

"Okay. Meet me at my car around 6?"

He looked perplexed.

"You need to sign some papers at the halfway house. I already talked to the manager."

William smiled, and it was the kind of grin that could have lit up the entire planet. He walked out of the cafeteria, and I noticed several women stared at him with mouths agape. It seemed as though I wasn't the only one digging his new makeover.

As sad and empty as I felt when William left the office, I realized that tomorrow Charlie would be coming home, and I'd have someone else to hold in my arms. Only this one was quite a bit smaller.

Chapter Nineteen

AMELIA

"Sugar and cream?" I called out to William as I turned on my Keurig.

Last night, I went with William to the local halfway house to fill out his paperwork and receive a copy of his key to the property and his own room. The manager, a woman in her mid-forties, was very kind and understanding of William's situation. She gave us a tour and showed him to his room. While much smaller than I'd hoped for him, it was a place to call his own. The manager, Wendy, advised that most of the other residents were recovering addicts and that William needed to be respectful of them and the house rules which included no illegal substances or alcohol.

William happily obliged, and for the first time in several years, he had a warm bed and the promise of safety and security.

This morning, I picked him up from the halfway house and brought him back to my apartment for breakfast. I learned to avoid asking William to eat in public places. Plus, I didn't mind cooking myself, even though my dishes were simple.

"Are you excited for Charlie to come home?"

"Very! I've missed him so much."

"I bet." William picked up a photograph of Charlie and me taken at his kindergarten graduation.

"You don't mind if I take you back home after breakfast, right?"

"Not at all."

"Charlie's never met any of my male friends," I said.

"You don't have to explain yourself, Amelia. I understand. Although, I would like to meet him some day."

My heart swelled. I hoped he could meet Charlie someday, too. I know Charlie would love William. And, now that William was all cleaned up, I wouldn't have to worry about my son asking those pesky, honest questions kids so often manage to do in public.

As I sipped the last few dregs of my vanilla biscotti-flavored coffee, someone knocked on my front door.

"Are you expecting someone?" William asked cautiously.

"No. Charlie's not supposed to be home for another couple of hours." I pulled myself up and walked to the door, peeking through the peephole.

There, on the other side of my door, stood my son and ex-husband, way earlier than planned.

"Who is it?" William whispered.

I turned around. "I'm sorry, William."

William stood like a deer caught in headlights, and I didn't blame him. This is *not* how this introduction was supposed to happen.

As soon as I unlocked the door, Charlie burst into the room with a smile and an extra inch or two.

"Hey, buddy!" He jumped into my arms, nearly knocking me over. "I missed you, too!"

Cal stepped into the apartment, and his eyes fell on William. He turned his nose up as though I had a skunk for a houseguest instead of a human being.

"Who're you?"

Charlie followed his father's eyes and looked at William, too. "Hi!"

My cheeks reddened darker than I ever thought possible as I tried to figure out how to explain my current predicament: my ex-husband, my son and my ex-vet, ex-homeless friend all in one room together.

"Uh, well—"

"My name is William. You must be Charlie?" He bent down and extended his hand.

Charlie looked at William's hand but eventually shook it. "Are you Mama's new boyfriend?"

I choked on air, and Cal gasped. William seemed to keep his cool, though. Must have been that military training shining through. "No, I'm a friend of your mom's. It's nice to meet you. I've heard all about you."

"Cool. Wanna play some video games with me?"

"Uh, sure."

Cal tapped his foot against the floor with his arms crossed over his body.

"Oh, yeah. Cal, this is William; William, this is Cal."

William extended his hand again only to have Cal look down as though he spit on it first. My ex turned to me. "I wish you would have told me you had a guest."

"I wish you would have told me you were dropping him off way ahead of schedule," I hissed.

Clenching my fists, anger rose inside me like a volcano about to erupt. Was I not allowed to have friends?

He scoffed, and I took a step toward him, except William was quicker.

"I'm William. It's nice to meet you." William let his hand drop back down to his side.

Cal looked him up and down with scathing eyes.

"Be nice, Cal," I spat. "You're going to be seeing William again soon, and you don't want ill will to ruin your special day."

"What are you talking about?" Cal asked as his eyes grew wide.

"William is going to be my wedding date," I taunted.

For a moment, I regretted blurting this out. I hadn't even asked William about coming with me. I hoped he wouldn't blow my cover. Luckily, he just stood by my side like the protector I never knew I needed.

"You've got to be kidding me?"

"Nope. Now, say goodbye to your son because you've outstayed your welcome here."

Cal sneered, and I hadn't abandoned the idea of punching him yet—I still had time. Even though we'd been divorced for a couple of years, he still knew how to push my buttons.

"Charlie! I'm leaving!"

"Bye, Dad," Charlie called from the other room.

I snickered at Cal's pained expression. Usually, I made Charlie hug his father goodbye if he got distracted by coming home, but not this time. He had our son for a whole two weeks; now it was my turn.

"See you next month!" I called out as Cal headed toward the elevator.

He didn't stop to turn around and acknowledge my promise, but I knew he was regretting ever inviting me to his wedding in the first place. That was worth receiving an invite, after all.

I closed the door and cringed as I turned around, now having to face another man in my life. I had no idea how William would act now that I'd practically used him to piss off Cal. Not that I didn't want him to come with me, because if he did, I wouldn't have to check single dinner, but it was gratifying to see Cal so fired up about a potential new man in my life.

"So," he began.

"Uh, yeah. About that." My cheeks reddened. "This is probably not happening in the right order, but will you be my date to a wedding in Candlebrook next month?" I smiled sweetly and batted my eyelashes, hoping the innocent vibe would motivate him to say yes.

"Do you want me to go because you genuinely want my company or to piss off your ex?"

"If I said both, would you still come with me?"

"Sure, why not?" He shrugged.

"Thank you!" I reached in for a hug and wrapped my arms around his neck. His fresh scent wafted into my nose and I closed my eyes tightly, wanting to absorb everything about his touch. With every passing day, William seemed to mind less and less when I embraced him. And I found myself wanting to provide comfort to him as often as I could. I truly cared about this man before me.

"I'm going to head out, though. Give you some time with Charlie."

"You want a ride?" I asked a little too eagerly.

"Nah, it's okay. I'll walk."

"Call me later. The halfway house has a phone, right?"

"Yup. See you later."

William left the apartment, and as soon as he closed the door, I felt a pang of sadness come over me. But I quickly remembered my number one guy was finally home.

The following day, William and I planned to take a shopping trip for new clothes for the both of us. Originally, I planned to have a sitter watch Charlie while we were gone, but he begged to come with us. In the history of being a mother to Charlie, never once has he pleaded to go clothes shopping. I had to take him up on the offer; who knew the next time he'd ask?

"Grab your iPad and anything else you want to bring along. We're leaving in about twenty minutes."

"Yes, Mama!" Charlie shouted from his bedroom.

In the short time Charlie was away, he already seemed a little bit more mature and carried a little less baby fat in his face. How did that happen? And how could I make it stop? I didn't want to think about my baby becoming a man, but I knew it would happen someday whether I liked it or not.

I packed a few bananas and bottles of water in my tote as a knock on the door rapped lightly.

"Come in!"

William opened the door, revealing large bags had taken residence under his eyes.

"Hey! Everything okay? You look a little tired."

"Didn't sleep much." He shrugged.

"Is there something wrong with the house?" Nerves crept into my consciousness. I worried how William would handle the new place.

"No, no. Not at all. Just... Not used to it yet."

I nodded and decided not to press any further.

Charlie burst out of his room and ran toward William, only to pump the brakes before he crashed right into him.

"Hiya, Charlie."

"Hey, William! Mama said we're going shopping. Are you going to buy new toys?"

William cracked a smile. "I wish, but I think the shopping might be a little boring."

"That's okay." Charlie shrugged and reached for the coat rack to grab his winter jacket. "Let's go!"

I'd never seen Charlie warm up to someone new so quickly. His comfort reduced my anxiety somewhat; I wasn't sure it was appropriate to have Charlie and William together so soon, but since they already met, a little more interaction couldn't hurt, right?

Ten minutes later, we were packed into my SUV and headed toward the outlet mall just outside of the city. I hadn't gone yet, but I figured it would be a great place to start with the basics. The drive took less than an hour, and the duration was spent listening to Charlie bombard William with questions. For once, I asked him to play his game and stop talking so much. I didn't want William to get annoyed with my kid the first day they spent together! I loved Charlie, but he was a persistent little bugger.

"What's your favorite movie? What's your favorite food? I like pizza, how about you?"

William seemed to get a kick out of him, which warmed my heart like a bowl of homemade chicken noodle soup. Or, at least he pretended to, which was fine for now.

When we arrived, I groaned loudly. It seemed as though

everyone and their mothers decided to come shopping today. William's demeanor also changed drastically as we parked the car. Droves of families headed toward the mall doors. I hadn't remembered William's shyness in public places. Silence washed over him as his body stiffened.

"Well, ready, everyone?"

Charlie bounced up and down, and William looked uneasy but nodded all the same.

"All right. Let's do this."

We chose to start the adventure with a trip into Macy's. Even though William specifically asked for a few new pieces of clothing, I thought he could use a new bed set, too. The halfway house was a great place for William to become accustomed to "normal" life again, but his room *was* a tad shabby. His sheets, gray and worn, looked as though they'd been used for several years. I didn't doubt they were clean, but a new set couldn't hurt.

"What about this one?" I showed him a soft turquoise comforter set with matching sheets.

He shrugged. "It's okay."

"Well, do you like it?"

William nodded solemnly, and I put it in the cart.

"Is everything okay?" I asked in a hushed tone.

"Yeah, why do you ask?"

"You just seem a little quiet is all. You still want to shop, right?"

"Yeah. Just tired."

"Sure." I narrowed my eyes, but he walked away. I knew something was up with William, but couldn't put my finger on it. Again, men are way more complicated than women. He made his way over to Charlie, who, much to my dismay, bounced up and down as he pointed toward a Superman bed set.

"Not today, kiddo," I scolded him gently and smiled.

William sighed and headed toward the living room section of

the store. He was about ten paces ahead of us when Charlie tugged on my coat.

"What is it?"

"Why is William sad?"

I cleared my throat. "Why do you think he's sad, honey?"

"I can tell by his eyes."

I'd seen the sadness too, though I wasn't entirely sure why he could be downtrodden today. It was a new beginning for him: new job, new place to live. I thought he'd be a little more comfortable in public places by now.

Around lunch time, we decided to load up the car with what we could for now and try to find a bite to eat. I saw a pizza place around the corner when we drove here, so I suggested it to the boys, and they happily agreed. The mall's food court appeared far too crowded. Not only did I want William to be comfortable, but I didn't want to wait in line for a half hour for a food court lunch.

The pizza place, small and family-owned, revealed the scent of wafting spices and fresh mozzarella. Family portraits covered the walls, and a toy machine with a mechanical crane stood in the corner beside an soda fountain.

"What would you like on your personal pan, Charlie?"

"Cheese, pineapple, and mushrooms!"

I wrinkled my nose, wondering where this kid came from. "Are you sure?"

"Duh, Mom. It's so good."

"You're the pickiest eater I know," I reminded him.

"It's good. I promise."

Where had he consumed those toppings on a pie before? Probably with Cal. He was poisoning his mind and taste buds.

"If you say so, but I don't wanna hear about how it's gross, and you want something else."

"I won't, Mama."

"What about you, William?"

"Uh, I'm not hungry." William stared at the floor.

"I thought you said you wanted pizza?" I swore I heard his stomach rumbling earlier.

"I did, but um, I don't have any money, and these prices are crazy."

"William, stop." I put my hand on his chest. "It's my treat."

"You're always treating me," he mumbled sourly.

"It's because I want to!"

"I'm not a charity case, Amelia!" He roared as a vein protruded in his forehead.

Patrons and workers alike turned to stare at the commotion. My stomach dropped as heat flooded to my cheeks.

"I don't think you're a charity case, William. I'm just trying to help," I whispered.

"Well, maybe you should stop. I don't deserve your help. I don't deserve any of this!" His voice rose over the hustle and bustle of the pizza parlor.

"Hey, don't yell at my Mama!" Charlie chirped.

William sighed and walked out of the pizza place toward the car. I wanted to go after him, but I couldn't leave Charlie. I figured he could use some space and fresh air, so I let him go. Charlie and I ate our pizza by the window just so I could keep an eye on William from the inside. He chose to sit by the car with his head in his hands. I wish I knew what he was thinking or what he was feeling, but truth be told, I couldn't. I'd never been homeless or a veteran. I had no idea what was going on inside his mind. I'm sure it couldn't be easy to adjust to a new and different life so quickly, but I was only helping him out of the goodness of my heart. He knew that? Right?

"I told you he was sad, Mama," Charlie said as he finished his last slice.

"I know, sweetie. I know he is."

"Did something bad happen to him?"

"Well, it's kind of complicated."

"I'm almost ten. I think I can handle it." He rolled his eyes.

Maybe he was right. I couldn't baby him forever. "William didn't have a home for a while."

"What do you mean?"

"He was living outside," I said carefully.

"Like in the cold?"

I nodded.

"Where would he sleep?"

"I'm not entirely sure, but I think he slept on a bench sometimes."

"That's sad." Charlie put his pizza crust down, and a tear slid down his cheek.

I pulled him into my lap. "It *is* sad, but wanna know what's great about William?"

"Huh?"

"He was in the Army, and he went to war. He's a hero and risked his life to keep us all safe."

"Wow!" Charlie said with his mouth agape. "Like Captain America?"

"Something like that." I smiled.

"He's my hero," Charlie said.

"Who is? Captain America?"

"No, Mama. William."

At that moment, I knew I was raising my son right, and my heart burst with love. Charlie and I shared something in common: William was my hero, too. Whatever he was dealing with now, we'd find a way to get through it together.

Chapter Twenty-One

WILLIAM

Spence died that day. He lost a lot of blood in the explosion and never recovered. Just like that, my trio of brothers became a duo. Luckily, no one else was hurt, but it wouldn't have mattered to me because once a heart breaks that deeply, it's impossible to feel any more pain.

Hudson and I promised to have each other's backs more than ever, if that was possible. We'd learned how life could be snuffed out in the blink of an eye. It was something I still couldn't comprehend even after dealing with my father's death. How could a person be living one second and cease to exist the next? How could someone be speaking and moving in one instant, and be wholly absent and immobile the next?

I missed Spence more than my heart could bear. Spence's death reopened the wounds of losing my father, and the memory of September 11th echoed in my mind. I always thought time would heal my wounds, but that was wishful thinking. There are some kinds of pain you simply never recover from. You'll carry the despair with you everywhere you go until it's your turn to die. Then, you'll be buried with it too.

Hudson and I continued our fight against terrorism, serving a few more tours overseas. Each day that passed, we grew tougher; our skin grew thicker, and we grew closer than ever. I would have died for him, and I know he would have died for me. Sure, we were thick as thieves with all other soldiers, too, but this was different. We had a bond that could not be duplicated.

Before our tour, Hudson met a nice girl back home. Her name was Maria, and they planned to marry once Hudson came home. Though the pregnancy was a surprise, Maria gave birth to a little girl she named Isabella while we were in Afghanistan. Apparently, their night before he deployed got a little crazy.

I couldn't have been happier for my best friend. Naturally, he named me Isabella's Godfather. He even bought me a Godfather tee shirt when he asked me. I said yes, and a new wave of pride entered my life. Even though I wouldn't meet her until I came home after the first tour, Isabella repaired a piece of my heart I thought would be damaged forever. Babies have a way of bringing life and light back into our lives even during the darkest of times.

However, darkness still hollowed my soul. Every year on my father's birthday, on Christmas, on my birthday, on the day of his death, and so many other holidays and anniversaries, I felt the full impact of his absence. And, my mother? If I was heartbroken, she was practically dead. A shell of her old self. My uncle wrote me letters as often as he could, and while I knew he attempted to sugarcoat the situation, I could tell my mother wasn't holding up well at all. Apparently, she wouldn't eat, sleep or leave the house.

I called when I could, but sometimes it was too hard to speak with her. She didn't sound like my mother; she didn't act like my mother. She was a stranger to me, a ghost of someone I once knew.

When I came home for a brief vacation during my first tour, my uncle wept in my arms. He told me he was trying his best to take care of my mom, but she was so far gone. I didn't blame him one bit. In fact, I didn't know how he managed to continue taking care of her. It broke my soul to look at her, let alone take care of her day in and day out. Her doctor prescribed her a heaping pile of antidepressants, but they only seemed to keep her low and sorrowful. Maybe her pain would never go away. Maybe this was just who she was now.

No matter what the reason, though, I couldn't bear it anymore. I couldn't stand to see my mother so melancholy and sullen. I tried every-thing I could to cheer her up while on leave. I cooked dinner, bought her flowers, offered to take her to art shows and museums, all her favorite things. That seemed like a past life, though. Or a dream. I couldn't remember the last time she smiled. I couldn't remember the last time my mom was happy. I suppose it would have been the morning before my father left for work for the very last time.

Soon, I grew angry with her. Didn't she know I'd lost my best friend? Didn't she know what I saw in Afghanistan? The terror? The death? Who was going to take care of me? Who was going to make sure I would get out of bed in the morning or eat breakfast? Not only did I nurse my wounds from war, but I had to nurse my mother, too. I hated myself for becoming so angry with her, but I couldn't help it. Life was fucked up.

I carried my depression with me everywhere. Every single day I thought about what could have been different in my life. Could I have saved Spence? Could I have saved my father? Why did I live and they died? I would have gladly traded places with either of them. I would have given my life to save them one hundred times over. But sometimes it doesn't matter how badly you want to turn back the clock, time keeps drag-ging us along regardless of our desire to hit pause or rewind.

In 2009, the eighth anniversary of the Twin Towers attack approached, as well as the end of my first enlistment in the Army. Most guys re-enlisted immediately. While my patriotism had never wavered since I'd enlisted, my desire for combat waned dramatically. Part of me felt numb to the death I encountered, and the other half of me screamed to escape. It was as though I applied a dab of lidocaine to my heart while simultaneously injecting it with a burst of adrenaline.

On the flight home, I had a layover a few hours away from the city.

"Hey, William. How's everything? Happy to be coming home?" Uncle Jimmy asked.

"Yeah, it'll nice to be back. How's Mom? Is she alright?"

"Well, see, that's what I'm calling about. I'm afraid I have some bad news."

My stomach lurched as I waited for my uncle to tell me I was an orphan.

"Your mom has been off lately. More than usual."

"What do you mean 'off?'"

"She forgets a lot of things. Last week, she thought I was your father. Another time, she left the oven on and almost burned the house down." His voice cracked with despair. "She's sick, William."

"What did the doctor say?"

"Early-onset Alzheimer's."

Alzheimer's? How was that possible? She was only in her mid-fifties. No, this couldn't be true.

"Are you sure? Did you get a second opinion?" My chest heaved.

"I'm sorry, kid. I took her to a handful of doctors who all said the same thing."

"I-I-I can't believe it."

"Me either."

It was then I made the second-most important decision after enlisting: I decided not to re-enlist. I needed to take care of my mom. I knew it wasn't fair for my uncle to handle the brunt of her care. Hell, he could use someone to help take care of him too. The guilt I carried after leaving my mother for war crushed my soul as though I carried the weight of the world on my shoulders. I needed to be a real man and take care of my mother, even if that meant foregoing my future in the military and leaving my brothers behind. Part of me knew I wasn't fit to fight either. Between the depression and anxiety I'd developed during the war and my mother, I realized I couldn't be in the military any longer.

When I told Hudson I wasn't going back, he understood. Sure, he was pissed, but he knew family came first.

Chapter Twenty-Two

AMELIA

William remained distant the entire ride home, not uttering a single word. I didn't want to force him to open up if he wasn't ready, but I also couldn't hide my disappointment at the day's turn of events. I honestly thought today would be fun and adventurous. It ended up being slightly disastrous instead. However, Charlie didn't seem to notice the awkwardness in the air and contently played his video game in the back seat. We stopped briefly at Kohl's so William could pick out a few additional pieces of clothing for work, but neither of us spoke while inside the department store. He quickly grabbed a few pairs of jeans, some boxer briefs, and some tee shirts.

When I parked the car outside of the halfway house, William mumbled a brief thank you, grabbed his new belongings and headed toward the front doors. Charlie called out goodbye, and William nodded and waved.

As much as I wanted to help William and comfort him, I knew he needed his space more than anything. I drove away as soon as William unlocked the door and disappeared into the halfway house, his new home.

Once I unlocked the door to our apartment, Charlie ran off to play in his room as per usual.

"Charlie!" I called out.

"Yeah, Mom?"

"I need to make a phone call. Play in your room for a little bit, okay?"

"'Kay!"

I stepped out onto my balcony and closed the door behind me. A frigid chill hung in the air, but I wanted to call William in private. Despite my best efforts to leave him be, I needed to know if he was okay.

"Hello?" I heard him sigh loudly on the other end of the call.

"Are you okay?" I sensed him building his wall back up, maybe higher than ever.

"I don't want to talk about it," he said coldly.

"Is there anything I can do to help? I hate seeing you like this."

For the most part, in my life, if there was a problem, I fixed it. If Charlie fell off his bike, I cleaned up the wound. If a client at work had a problem, I took on the case. William? I had no idea what to do or how to help him. It felt like every time I tried to get close to him, he pushed me away.

"Yeah, well, I hate feeling like this."

"Feeling like what?" My heart thumped wildly in my chest.

"Like I don't deserve this second chance."

"You of all people deserve a second chance," I urged and wished he realized this, too.

"I don't know how to handle this," he said.

"Handle what?" I asked softly.

"All of this. This halfway house, the new stuff, the job. You're too nice to me. I don't deserve any of it."

"William, you've had a hard time, and life didn't go your way for a while, but I'm doing all this because I care about you. I don't pity you or feel bad for you. I genuinely want to help you start over and get your life back."

"Why do you care so much, though?" His voice broke.

"I feel like we've gotten to know each other really well. I genuinely care about you, and I want you in my life. I want to help you any way I can. And please stop saying you don't deserve this. You deserve all the good things life has to offer."

"Well, please don't buy me anything else. I want to be able to provide for myself going forward."

"Okay, I'll back off. But I'm here if you need anything," I said genuinely. I wished more than anything he'd let me help him. I wanted him to know how much I cared. Even though he hadn't meant to, he weaseled his way into my heart.

"Thank you. I do appreciate it, even if I don't always act like I do."

"Everyone needs a helping hard at first. I just happen to have two helping hands to give you." I hoped he heard the smile in my voice.

"I'm happy I met you, Amelia," he said quietly.

"Me, too."

We didn't talk for a few moments, then I changed the subject. "Big day tomorrow."

"Yup."

"You ready to start work again?" I asked cheerfully.

"I think so. I'm kinda nervous, though."

"You're going to do great," I reassured him.

"That's what I thought at my last few jobs."

"May I ask what happened?"

"Well, a few of them were construction jobs. You know, under the table gigs? The loud noises and fast pace weren't for me," he trailed off.

I thought back to when I woke him up and he pulled out a knife. I could only imagine the dark thoughts clouding his mind. It didn't take an expert psychologist to understand some jobs simply wouldn't be a good fit for him. I hoped this maintenance job would be different.

"I'm making dinner tonight. Would you care to join us?"

"I think they serve dinner here," William said slowly.

"Well, Charlie and I would love to have you over here. I can send a Lyft for you?"

"Sure. I just need to shower first."

———

William whipped together a delicious helping of spaghetti for Charlie and me, and I have to admit, it was nice having someone cook for *me* for a change. Even though I said I'd cook, William took over kitchen duties for the evening. He even let Charlie help pour the sauce and stir it all together. William apologized to Charlie for acting distant earlier and promised to make it up to him by playing whichever game he wanted on XBox. As soon as Charlie heard, "XBox" he forgot about the day's turn of events and dove toward his controller.

Once dinner was ready, though, I reminded Charlie to turn the XBox off, and we all sat together at the kitchen table. It felt wonderful to have a sort-of family dinner again. Cal, Charlie and I had our last meal as a family a very long time ago. I'd forgotten how nice it was to sit at the table, sip wine and have company. Soft jazz crooned from the speakers in the background while snow gently fell from the sky.

"Mama said you're a soldier," Charlie said as he slurped a noodle.

"Manners, Charlie."

"Sorry, Mama."

"Your Mom wasn't lying, but I'm not in the Army anymore."

"What happened?" Charlie asked.

I held my breath and glanced at William, then Charlie and back again.

"You want to know?" William asked skeptically.

"Yeah!"

"I was an infantry soldier," William said.

"Cool, what kinds of stuff did you do?"

I watched as William breathed deeply and closed his eyes.

"Charlie, I think we should talk about something else."

"Did you kill people?" Charlie asked curiously.

"Charlie!"

"It's okay, Amelia," William interjected. "I don't mind."

"Well, it's not an appropriate conversation at the dinner table."

"Your mother's right. Sorry, kid. Maybe another time." Tension slid off his shoulders like ice.

"Aw! Come on, Mom! I just want to know this one thing!"

"Not today, Charlie," I said with my "mom" voice.

"You're no fun." He pouted.

"I know I'm the meanest mom in town, huh? And, since I'm so mean, I guess you don't want me to make brownies for dessert."

"Brownies?" His eyes lit up.

"Too bad," I feigned.

"No, Mom! You're cool! Now please make brownies."

I giggled and collected the dirty dishes. "Fine, but you gotta help with the dishes."

"Anything for brownies."

William and I shook our heads.

Once the dishes were rinsed and put in the dishwasher with Charlie's help, I started the magical process of making my world-famous brownies. Okay, maybe they weren't "world-famous," but they always sold out at the school bake sales.

Charlie helped crack the eggs, which may or may not have been a huge mistake. He accidentally dropped three of them on the kitchen floor. William showed him how to crack an egg properly, and Charlie oohed and awwed once he'd done it himself.

"Mom, baking is fun!"

William poured the brownie batter into the pan and put it in the oven. There was still a respectable amount of batter in the mixing bowl, though, and William swiped the side with his pinky.

"This is my favorite part," he said.

"Hey, give me some of that batter!" I demanded with a smile.

William took the batter on his pinky and slowly brought it to my lips. I was about to put my mouth on his finger when he quickly moved it and wiped the batter on my nose.

"Hey!" I called out.

William burst into laughter, and it was the first time he ever grinned this broadly. His smile warmed my heart and left me wanting to leap into his arms. His happiness echoed around the kitchen, and suddenly, my apartment felt like a home.

In that moment, a different kind of happiness splashed inside my heart. All the time I spent with William, I knew we made great friends, but could there be something more to our story? Could *we* ever be something more? Yes, we came from different backgrounds, but were we all that different? We both loved our country; we both lost our fathers far too soon, and we enjoyed spending time together. Would that be enough? Would he ever see me as more than just a friend? There was also the fact I have a child. William only just started sleeping in a bed instead of a bench; he couldn't be ready to be a stepfather yet.

He scraped more batter from the bowl, and I grabbed his hand so he couldn't trick me again. With a mischievous grin, I licked his finger clean.

William's face flushed, and his eyes bulged. My heart thudded against my rib cage and butterflies fluttered inside my belly. Was there something else here? There had to be!

"Yum!" My tongue darted out to clean off my lips as I shot him a dazzling smile.

"You're crazy," he whispered with a grin.

"Hopefully the good kind of crazy?" I asked hopefully.

"That's debatable." He winked.

We spent the rest of the evening cracking jokes, comparing favorite movies and books, and even managed to squeeze in a game of tag with Charlie. As William jumped over the sofa and alluded my desperate son around the living room, my heart filled to the brim with joy. Once Charlie finally caught William and tagged him, William charged after me, and I let him catch me.

Chapter Twenty-Three

AMELIA

"Ready for your big day?" I asked, looking over at William, who was seated next to me.

"Amelia, you realize I'm just maintenance, not a rocket scientist, right?"

"Yeah, yeah. But, you should still be excited. Plus, we get to work together!" I imagined meeting each other for lunch and taking walks together once the weather broke.

"Well, not together, together. You're an attorney, and I'm not."

"You're salting my game this morning, William."

"Mom? What's 'salting my game' mean?" came the voice from the backseat.

I chuckled from the front seat as we drove Charlie to school. I picked up William on the way to Charlie's elementary school so we could drive to work together, too. "It means like bumming me out or raining on my parade."

"So, when you take away my iPad you're like salting my game?"

"Exactly, buddy." I looked in the rearview mirror and witnessed Charlie smirking in the backseat. Such a little stinker.

I also couldn't help but steal glances at William out of the corner of my eye. He'd styled his freshly cut hair, and his beard grew in nicely. I wanted to reach across and touch his face. After the brownie batter "incident," no other instances of touching came about. Maybe I'd imagined the electricity between us?

However, I couldn't remember ever feeling this attracted to a person, not even Cal. Sure, I was attracted to Cal while we were married, but in the "shrugs my shoulders, he's not that bad" kind of way. With William, it was completely different. Lately, when I saw him, warmth in my belly spread rapidly enough to nudge my heart incessantly and make my brain go fuzzy. I never knew it was possible to experience such a strong pull to another human being, besides my son, of course.

I found myself thinking of William constantly and counting down the seconds until I could see him again. And, no, it wasn't just because his makeover revealed a bright and shiny penny under the layers of street weariness. I felt a pull toward him even before all that. Maybe we were always destined to meet, like fate or something.

We dropped Charlie off at school and giggled as he sprinted toward his group of friends like a lost puppy reuniting with the litter.

"Ready for work?"

"As I'll ever be."

William and I walked into the office together and stayed close as we fought the wind every step of the way. Even though February was half over by now, winter didn't seem to show any signs of leaving town.

William opened the door for me, and I bowed. "Thank you, sir."

"You're such a nerd," he teased.

Our Human Resources Coordinator stood at the receptionist's desk, waiting for William to arrive. I'd learned it was customary to have someone from HR greet you on your first day and walk you to training, except for the attorneys who seemed to be thrown into the wolves' den right away.

"Have a great morning. Meet for lunch around noon in the cafeteria?"

"Sounds good." William smiled weakly, and I sensed his nerves. I knew he'd be okay, though. I mean the man served in the military after all. I'm sure this job would be a walk in the park compared to war.

That morning, I had an urgent meeting with Leo Brass regarding his case. After weeks of pouring over the details, we were positive his accountant had been stealing the company's profits and depositing them in offshore accounts. However, even though it seemed like a slam dunk, I had to prep Leo for civil court, where he could be called to testify.

"Morning, darlin'," Leo said as he bent down to kiss my hand.

"Nice to see you again, Leo. I have some excellent news!"

We took our respective seats in the conference room near my office, and I delved into the details of the upcoming civil case.

"So, the accounting firm we hired to help with the numbers discovered a handful of instances that several thousands of dollars disappeared each month over the course of ten to twelve years."

"Bastard!" Leo exclaimed. "I knew it was bad, but I didn't know it was this bad. What's the damage?"

"Well, it looks like he stole about two mil over the course of his time with your company. We believe we may have found the accounts, too. I have a few contacts who will be traveling to the banks on the islands where the financial institutions may be located."

"Good!" Leo pounded his fist on the conference room table.

"We're going to ask the judge to force him to pay back the money he stole, but also to pay your legal fees as we wouldn't be in this mess if it weren't for him to begin with."

"You're a rock star; you know that, Amelia?"

"Oh, stop!" Heat resinated my cheeks.

"So, what do I have to say on the stand if they call me up?"

"Nothing crazy. Just confirm how long Roy's been working for you and when you suspected he might be involved with the missing money situation."

"You know, I heard rumors he's going to say I coerced him or blackmailed him into stealing the money for myself." Leo shifted uncomfortably in the noir leather chair.

"That would require solid proof. A judge wouldn't just take his word for it. It's not true, right?" I asked, trailing off.

"Of course not!" he insisted.

"Sorry, Leo. I had to ask." I reached out and patted his hand with mine.

"No worries at all, my dear."

We concluded the meeting, then Leo kissed me sweetly on the cheek goodbye. I sincerely hoped he was telling the truth about the accounts, because there was nothing more embarrassing than being caught with your pants down in a courtroom. Well, err, in my case, it'd be a skirt.

I glanced at my watch around five to noon, and my heart fluttered with excitement. I couldn't wait to hear about William's day thus far and eat lunch together. Now I'd have a real friend at work. Of course, I had Karen, but she was more like a mother figure to me. William was different.

I scurried to the elevator and rapidly pressed the button for the ground floor where our cafeteria was located. My breathing quickened, and my pulse raced as I saw the back of William across the room. I wanted to run to him until I saw another woman, whom I'd never met, hug him tightly. My heart sank faster than the Titanic.

The woman, blonde, busty and tiny threw her arms around William and screeched like a little girl.

Did they know each other? She looked familiar. I knew she was an attorney, but we hadn't crossed paths yet.

I saw her face light up as they sat and talked at a table with only two chairs.

Now what?

Do I go over and interrupt them? Or, do I leave them alone? William caught my eye and waved me over. Well, now I didn't have a choice.

"Hi, William," I said.

"Amelia, this is Lucy. Lucy, this is Amelia. Lucy and I went to high school together."

I extended my hand toward her, and she returned the gesture airily. "It's nice to meet you," I offered. "I don't think we've met yet. I'm in the corporate practice."

"I'm in environmental." She yawned.

"I bet that's exciting. I've heard many good things about that practice."

Lucy nodded and dug into her sushi platter. She didn't seem very interested in conversing, and I took that as my cue to leave.

"Well, I'll let you two finish catching up."

"Wait, why don't you join us for lunch? We did have plans," William offered sweetly.

As much as I wanted to catch up and hear all about William's day, a nagging voice in my head reminded me I had a few more cases to continue preparing for.

"That's okay. I think I'll have a working lunch today. Very busy."

"I'll call you later, okay?" William asked.

"Sure, sounds fine."

I stood in line and ordered the special for the day: chicken souvlaki salad. I waved goodbye to William and returned to my office to eat and research. I spent most lunch breaks poring over documents and cases.

"You really should take a real break one of these days," Karen said, poking her head into my office.

"I know," I groaned. "But I have so much to do."

"It will be here after your lunch hour, dear!"

"Always looking out for me, Karen."

"You bet I am!"

I took a bite of my salad and wondered how William faired downstairs. I sensed a hint of chemistry between him and his friend, Lucy. Maybe they dated in high school? I tried to push the twinge of jealousy from my mind and worked well into the evening, as usual.

Chapter Twenty-Four

AMELIA

At four o'clock the next day, Karen stepped into my office with a pleading look on her face.

"Hey, Karen. What's up?"

"I wanted to ask you a favor," she replied hesitantly.

"Anything."

"There's a work happy hour tonight, and I was wondering if you'd come with me."

"Huh? I didn't know there was a work happy hour." I furrowed my brow.

"I sent you the invite on Outlook last week," Karen said.

I scrolled through my messages and lo and behold, there was the invite. I'd skipped over it in a mad rush to respond to all my messages the previous Wednesday.

"I don't think I can make it. I have to prep for Leo's case."

"You already have everything worked out. I looked at the files! Plus, you could use a little fun."

"How do you know?" I teased.

"Because I sit right out there and rarely see you get up from your desk, missy!"

"I don't know," I said carefully.

"You really should come. It's an attorney event, and it will give you the chance to meet the others in different practice areas."

She had a point; I hadn't met everyone yet. Being introduced to Lucy the day before was a prime example of me needing to expand my network.

"I'll be ready about five fifteen as long as I can get a sitter."

When I moved here, I found a few sweet college-aged girls in the neighborhood who said they'd watch Charlie anytime I needed them. I wasn't sure if I could trust them, being so young and at the age when partying can be a top priority, but both girls proved to be diamonds in the rough. Sometimes, trials ran longer than I expected, and it was a relief to know I'd found reliable help. Plus, it didn't hurt that Charlie had a crush on both girls even though he was adamant they had "cooties."

"Hi, Carrie? Yes, would you mind watching Charlie tonight? I have a work thing."

"No problem, Amelia. Do you need me to pick him up from school?"

"That would be perfect! I'll call and let them know you'll be there to grab him instead of me. Thanks again!"

I gave Karen the thumbs up from my office, and she smiled gleefully.

At half after five, Karen and I rushed into the bar and out of the cold for the happy hour. Our rosy cheeks disappeared in the dim lighting of the establishment, and we saw the group of attorneys and a few paralegals gathered in the corner. Some I knew; some I wanted to meet, and most I couldn't put a name to.

Miniature chandeliers hung from the delicate ivory ceilings, and a saxophone player crooned in the corner. The windows were tinted so pedestrians couldn't leer inside. Most patrons were dressed in business suits and skirts, and even the waitstaff and bartenders wore bow ties. The air reeked of superiority and money.

"I'll get us something to drink. What would you like?" I asked Karen.

"Oh, I'll just have whatever you're having." She scurried off to jabber with her other work friends while I stood at the bar and waited to grab the bartender's attention. I had a crisp twenty dollar bill in my hand which, when it caught his eye, brought him right over to me.

"What can I get for you?"

"Two glasses of Pinot Grigio, please." The bartender, young and handsome, winked at me as he poured the wine into glasses.

"On the house." He smiled.

"Wow, thank you!" I left him the twenty on the bar, anyway. I believed in tipping graciously.

I joined Karen and the other attorneys in the group. Karen introduced me to the dozen or so lawyers, and all seemed happy to finally meet me. Then, Lucy appeared with a glass of red wine and a toothy, white smile upon her flawless face.

"Amelia, you made it," she said.

"Mhmm. What are you drinking?" I asked awkwardly. Still confused about the nature of her relationship with William, my thoughts turned jumbled and blurry around her.

"The house red. It's to *die* for," she cooed.

I nodded and smiled politely before turning around to converse with another attorney, whom I recognized as being in my same practice. I felt Lucy's eyes watching me, but I tried to ignore the anxiety rumbling in my belly.

Amelia Montgomery wasn't the jealous type, so why was I feeling so envious of this woman? I was strong, intelligent, and a good mom—I shouldn't doubt myself. I tried my best to push away the thoughts of Lucy and focus on my other colleagues. After all, we'd be working together, and Lucy and I might not ever collaborate on a case.

At about seven o'clock, my body jolted as I remembered there was one more piece of research I'd wanted to finish before the day's end. Panic swept across my mind as I realized I needed to cut the evening short and return to the office.

"Amelia!" Karen whined. "Tonight was supposed to be about less work and more socializing!"

"I know, but I need to go back. I only have the sitter for a few more hours. I could use the extra time to work."

"Don't think this is your 'get out of jail free card,'" Karen said, her eyes narrowed.

"Yes, Mom," I teased.

After a quick goodbye to the other attorneys, I walked briskly back to the office and spent the new few hours in the firm's library. Part of me wished I could let myself enjoy a few drinks with co-workers, but the other, louder part of me knew this is where I needed to be.

No one prepares you for having a parent with Alzheimer's. No one taught me how to react when my mother couldn't recognize me. There wasn't a course in school, or an FYI in a newsletter sent to my email account. I was all on my own. Uncle Jim returned home after I moved back in. As time wore on, he'd developed his own need for care: he'd fallen a few months back, and the injury required a hip replacement. Even though the recovery time wasn't very long, I knew I couldn't ask him to be the man of my house any longer. He did his part, and now it was time to do mine.

My days consisted of waking my mother around eight in the morning for breakfast. Every morning, I cooked eggs, toast, and bacon; it used to be her favorite. Most days, though, she refused to eat. Some days, she threw her tray at me, and on rare occasions, she hid it under her pillow. I couldn't trust her to eat a meal without causing some sort of trouble. Sometimes, I spoonfed her because she refused to use the utensils. Others, I watched her chew and swallow every bite. She also tended to hoard her pills. Her doctor prescribed a sedative for when her outbursts grew uncontrollable. A few times, though, I found a stash of the medicine under her pillow. I didn't know why she did this, and she probably didn't know why, either.

I saved a good amount of money while serving considering I didn't own a house, a car or have a family. But now that my mother was my main priority, most of the money I'd saved went to her care. The money my father left us went toward the mortgage and other bills; however, he didn't leave as much money for us as I presumed. I had no guesses as to where most of his money went, and I was afraid to dig into the matter in case something I found tarnished his memory. I couldn't help but feel angry, though. All those hours he worked late, and what did he have to show for it? But, I embraced my new life and worked my damndest to take care of my mom.

Outside of caring for my mother, my entire life stood at a standstill. Hudson continued to serve, and while we stayed in communication, it wasn't quite the same after I left the military. I didn't have time to go out socialize, make new friends, or even find a woman. My days consisted of taking care of my mom from sun up to sun down and all the time in between.

I talked to a girl I met online. We emailed every day, but she grew annoyed when I couldn't meet up in person. I explained to her about my mother having Alzheimer's, but I couldn't ask her to wait around forever. We stopped talking after a few months, and the loneliness crept back in.

One morning, when I woke my mom up for breakfast, she peered at me differently than usual.

"William? Is that you?"

My heart leaped out of my chest.

Was she lucid?

"Mom? Do you know who I am?"

She studied me carefully. "What's going on? Something doesn't feel right."

The doctors told me this was possible, that on a random day, at a random time, she could become herself again. But there was no way to tell how long it would last.

I sat down beside her on the bed and pulled her into a tight embrace. "I've missed you, Mom."

"Missed me? Where have you been? When did you get back from your tour?"

"This is going to be hard to hear, but I have to tell you something."

"What is it, sweetie?" The familiar twinkle in her eyes shattered me. I wanted to bottle up this moment to keep until the day I died.

"Mom, you have Alzheimer's. I left the service to take care of you. This is the first time you've recognized me in a very long time."

Tears streamed down her cheeks, and she sobbed on my shoulder. "I'm so sorry, Son. I never wanted to put you through this. I love you."

"I love you, too. I'm here for you, okay?"

"Are you married? Do you have kids? I feel like I'm missing out on your entire life." She wept.

"No. I'm not married, and I don't have kids."

"Are you seeing anyone?" Hope hung on her words.

I looked at her sorrowfully.

"You don't have time to meet a nice girl, do you?"

"I like taking care of you. I don't mind."

She nodded, understanding her role in my life. For eighteen years, she took care of me, and now that I was all grown up, I took care of her.

"You shouldn't have to live like this," she croaked between sobs.

"It's my choice, Mom!"

"You should put me in a home."

"Never. I'm here for you."

Then, she whispered, "I miss your father, but I suppose if I don't know who I am, I can't miss him while I'm sick. Right?"

I nodded.

"Maybe there is a silver lining in this whole thing."

For the next two hours, we caught up. I told her a few war stories, and we reminisced about my father, too. It felt like I had my mom back, but I knew it was temporary, and so I cherished every single second. Once the sun began to set, though, a pang of confusion struck her, and I knew it was time... Time to say goodbye.

"Where am I?" she asked suddenly.

"Mom, you're home. You're safe."

"William? What's going on? Who are you?"

"It's me, Mom."

She reached out and cupped my face in her hands. "Why are you here?"

I nodded as a tear fell down my cheek and landed on her hand.

"I want to sleep, William, but I feel antsy. May I have my medicine?"

I unlocked her nightstand and pulled out the medicine bottle. I glanced around and realized her glass of water stood empty on her dresser. I stood to refill the glass.

"I'll be right back, Mom. Will you be okay for a minute?"

"Yes, dear." She waved me off.

I returned a few minutes later with a fresh glass of ice-cold water. However, my mom had already fallen asleep.

She must have been more tired than she thought. Probably from the excitement of remembering.

That night, I lay in bed and contemplated my life. I missed my dad; I missed Spence, and I missed Hudson. I missed the life I hadn't lived yet, and I missed being a soldier. I felt as though time was passing me by, and I couldn't catch up. My life felt like a speeding train disappearing down the tracks and out of view. Would I ever be in control of my life again?

———

The following morning, my alarm woke me at seven in the morning. I realized my mom slept through the night without waking up. Most nights, she woke up once or twice, confused and angry. Last night, though, she didn't.

I went to her room, and she lay there, motionless.

"Mom, it's time to wake up. You've been sleeping a long time."

She didn't move. Her chest didn't rise. Her skin appeared blue and life-less. Dread flooded my entire body as I knelt beside her. She wanted peace. She didn't want to be a burden to me anymore. Out of the corner of my eye, I noticed the pill bottle still on the nightstand; I never put it away. When I picked it up, it was empty. Not one single pill remained.

My father died, Spence died, and now my mother was another body to add to the list of the deceased. I'd never felt so alone in my life.

———

You know the saying, "Money doesn't grow on trees?" Well, it's true. My mother's funeral cost thousands upon thousands of dollars, which drained my checking account. Then, I received a handful of medical bills in the mail for my mother's treatment and appointments, which took hold of my savings account. Not only did I feel as though I was spiritually drowning, but now I was overwhelmed with bill after bill after bill.

The job market was tough in New York, too. I couldn't find a job anywhere, not even McDonald's. Oh, and I tried everywhere, believe me. I even went as far as to beg the local schools for a janitorial position. None were hiring. In a few short months, I went from being a badass soldier to a jobless orphan. I had held the world at my fingertips, and now the world crushed me with its unforgiving wrath.

If my father's passing was the worst day of my life, and my mother's and Spence's deaths followed closely, the next worst day came when I checked the mail on a sweltering August morning. The letter from our bank advised our mortgage was in default, and I had thirty days to leave before the bank foreclosed on the house. When I finished reading the letter, I broke out in hysterical laughter. I laughed so hard I cried and then continued until my belly hurt. Was this my life now?

I could have called Uncle Jimmy and asked for the money, but he'd done enough to help me and my family. I couldn't put the burden of a loan on his shoulders, too.

Not wanting to spend the next thirty days waiting for my home to be taken away from me, I sold what I could and packed up the rest of my belongings, which were minimal. I kept family photo albums, my mother's jewelry, and a few other random keepsakes.

For a few months, I crashed with various friends from school. However, this wasn't a permanent solution. Without a job, I couldn't afford an apartment, and without an apartment, I couldn't find a job. During the interviews I'd been afforded, the hiring managers asked about my permanent address since I'd left it blank on my applications. Once I told them my situation, I never heard back. It was a revolving door of rejections. It didn't take long to run out of friends to stay with. It didn't take long to realize I only had one option left: to live on the streets.

Chapter Twenty-Six

AMELIA

As the weeks passed, my hours at work only increased. William and I saw less and less of each other, which tore through me every time I saw him in the halls of the office. I wanted to stay and chat, but I had work to do. Our firm had been hired to represent a large European corporation wanting to extend their business to America. It took myself and a handful of other attorneys to manage the matter.

Another noticeable change in my life came by way of my son and his increased temper tantrums. It seemed as though every other day he defied me or caused some sort of trouble, whether at home or school. Charlie's teacher wrote me a less than pleasant email about my son's behavior in class. She said he'd grown rude and disruptive during school hours. Bewilderment coursed through my mind: this wasn't my son; this wasn't how I raised Charlie to act. I even had to confiscate the iPad until Charlie cleaned up his act. Sure, I realized he was a kid, but he knew better.

One particular work night, I arrived home past midnight. Carrie, the babysitter, startled as I opened the door. She stretched and rubbed her eyes. "Hi, Ms. Montgomery."

"Sorry I'm so late, Carrie." I didn't bother coming up with an excuse; it was the same reason I always had: I got distracted at work and lost track of time.

I handed her a generous stack of bills and ordered a Lyft to take her home.

"How was he tonight?"

"He was a tad emotional," she said awkwardly.

"Emotional?"

"He had trouble falling asleep. He was crying and calling out for you."

Her words formed a metaphorical knife, piercing my heart. "Oh," was all I managed to say.

"Goodnight," Carrie said and left as her ride pulled up outside.

"Night, Carrie."

My baby boy cried for me? Could this be the source of all the bad behavior he'd developed recently? Was he just vying for my attention, whether it was good attention or bad? I remembered being Charlie's age and wondering why my father worked so far away. I'd wondered why he worked so late and rarely came home. Was I turning into my father? Would Charlie grow up to have a borderline unhealthy work ethic like me and my father before me?

Dizziness invaded my mind, and I needed a glass of wine, STAT.

I opened a bottle of Riesling and glanced at the calendar on our refrigerator. Tomorrow, Charlie's school was putting on their annual play. This year's production was *Peter Pan*. Charlie rehearsed endlessly for a part, which shocked me to my core. I never knew he was interested in theatre, but then again, there seemed to be a lot of clues I'd missed in my home as of late. Charlie got the leading part and was cast as Peter Pan.

I put a note in my phone about the play so I wouldn't miss it. My plan was simple: I'd only stay a little bit after work hours, then I'd head immediately to Charlie's school for the play at six o'clock in the evening. Karen offered to pick Charlie's costume up at the dry cleaners and bring it to him at school. I wouldn't have the time to do so myself.

"You're a lifesaver, Karen!"

"It's not a problem at all, dear. I'm excited to see Charlie!"

Karen didn't have any grandchildren of her own, and I sensed her excitement at having a new child in her life to dote upon. Karen morphed into much more than my secretary since I'd started working at the firm; she was like a mother, too. Which meant she was like a grandmother to Charlie.

That night, I fell asleep at my desk with a case file on my chest. I slept for a few hours before my phone alarm woke up me, making me jolt straight into the air at its incessant beeping.

Charlie trotted out of his room, fully clothed and ready for school. "Morning, champ."

"Hi, Mom."

"Tonight's the big night! Are you ready?"

"Yeah, I guess so. I'm kind of nervous." He fidgeted with his shirt.

"You'll be great, I already know it," I said, my face aglow.

"What if I forget a line?"

"Then just improvise!"

"Okay, if you say so." Charlie bit his lip anxiously.

I stood and walked over to my son, kissing his forehead and ruffling his hair. "I believe in you, kid."

He smiled and wrapped his tiny, yet strong arms around my waist.

"You're coming, right?"

"Wouldn't miss it for the world! You kiddin' me?"

"William is coming, too," he said matter-of-factly.

"He is?"

"Yeah, I invited him."

Damn, I never thought of inviting William myself. Probably because we hadn't had the time to catch up recently.

"How did you invite him?" I quizzed my darling son.

"Well, I looked up the number to the halfway house and called him."

"You did?" I asked incredulously.

"Yeah, Mom. It was easy."

"You're too smart!"

He shrugged and poured himself a bowl of cereal.

"I'm going to take a quick shower, get dressed and then we can go, okay?"

Charlie stuck up his thumbs and winked at me. I couldn't help but giggle to myself. It was the best morning we'd had in over a week. Maybe things would turn around now? I sure hoped so. It's possible the stress of the play caused Charlie to act out, at least it seemed to be the case.

———

The day wore on as any other day at work. I met with a few clients, worked on a few proposals, and researched future cases. I ate lunch at my desk again, and only stopped when a visitor knocked on my office door.

"Come in!"

William waltzed into my office and whistled. "Wow-ee, this is some office!"

My cheeks turned pink. "Thanks! It's good to see you. How have you been?"

"Well, if you bothered to step away from your desk and have lunch with me, you'd know," he teased.

"I know, I know. I'm sorry. It's just I'm so—"

"Busy?"

"Uh, yeah," I answered.

"You're working yourself to death," William said more seriously.

"Just don't want to disappoint Ross or my clients," I replied sheepishly.

"So, I'll be seeing you at Charlie's play tonight?"

"The what?" I skimmed a file in front of me while I took a taste of my soup.

"*Peter Pan?* Your child's first theatrical performance?"

"Right! The play! Of course I'll be there." I cringed at my forgetfulness.

"You know, Charlie is afraid you'll forget about it."

"He is?" My heart plunged into my stomach.

"Yeah, he told me on the phone when he called me. You can't miss this, Amelia."

"I won't," I said way more defensively than I intended. "How's work?"

"It's going well." He appeared genuinely happy and at ease. It was a nice change of pace for him and he looked well.

"Any issues?"

"Not at the moment."

"Happy to hear it!"

Silence crept into the conversation as we sat awkwardly together. "Well, I've got to get back to work. See you tonight?"

William's eyes narrowed. "Yeah, I hope so." He strolled out of my office and glanced back in my direction before disappearing from view.

At half past four, Karen popped into my office. "Hey, you. I'm heading out to grab Charlie's costume and then go to the school. You'll be there on time, right? I'll be saving you a seat in the front row."

"Yes," I replied absentmindedly. "See you soon."

Just before Karen stopped in, Ross visited me, too. My office felt like the place to be today, I could barely concentrate with all my colleagues popping by.

"Amelia?"

"Hi, Ross. How's everything?"

"Good. Good. How's the proposal going for Hershel, Inc.?"

"Not bad. I still have a few more docs to pull and look over."

"Can you have that ready for me by tomorrow morning?"

I glanced at my calendar. "I thought it's due next Wednesday?"

Ross sighed. "It was, but I need it earlier. Think you can manage?"

As if I didn't already have a heaping load of work at my feet. "Sure, I'm on it." I couldn't let Ross down. Plus, I was still the newest partner at the firm and felt I needed to prove my worth. My father once told me if your boss asks for you to do something, you need to have it done before they walk out the door. He burned that mentality into me at a very young age.

I grabbed a cup of coffee from the lounge on my floor and returned to my desk, which was beginning to feel like a prison. Maybe I *was* working too hard? Shaking away the feeling of doubt about my work ethic, I put the pedal to the metal and got to work.

Despite a few more cups of coffee, my eyelids drooped while I scanned another pile of documents before me. The sun set by now, and I had a sinking feeling I was forgetting something. Before I had the time to try and remember, my head drooped, and I slid back in my chair, sound asleep.

Chapter Twenty-Seven

AMELIA

"Amelia? Amelia?"

I opened my eyes and wiped away a stream of drool from the corner of my mouth.

Where was I?

Then, as if a jolt of lightning shot through me, I sat upright, my heart plunging deep into my chest.

William stood before me, arms crossed and a look of fury upon his face. I'd never seen such a scathing look in his eyes before. I glanced at my watch; it read 9:07. Then, I remembered what I'd forgotten before I abruptly fell asleep. Tonight was Charlie's play.

"Oh, my god!" I cried.

"Yeah. You forgot about Charlie. Your only son." Distaste crept into his tone.

I flew out of my chair and grabbed my coat, but William blocked the doorway.

"I need to go home! Is he there? Holy shit! I can't believe I fell asleep. I set my alarm and everything." Panic poured from my voice.

"Charlie is at Karen's house," William said coolly.

"Please move. I need to go get him!"

"He doesn't want to see you, Amelia."

Tears sprang from my eyes. "What do you mean?"

"I watched your son look at your empty seat all night long. Every other kid had parents waiting for them after the play, except for Charlie."

I crumbled to the ground, shuddering as the tears flowed freely down my cheeks. Shame and bile rose in my throat, and I couldn't bear to imagine the pain Charlie felt at this very moment. How could I have let him down like this? I set an alarm and everything!

"You hurt your son tonight. You really messed up."

"I know, I know!" I rocked back and forth, my knees pulled to my chest.

William knelt down beside and put an arm around my shoulders. "What's going on? Why are you working yourself so hard here?"

"I can't help it, William. All I think about is work. I don't want to let anyone down."

"Well, I hate to break it to you, but you're letting down your son. And me."

"You?" I sniffled.

"I miss you. We rarely see each other or talk anymore. I thought... I thought I could count on you to be there if I needed you, but now I don't know."

"My father, he taught me to be dedicated to my work. He didn't want me to live my life poor like I did growing up. He wanted better for me and my family."

"Don't you see? You already *are* providing for your family. You don't need to work eighty hours a week to do so. You've gone past the point of success and are heading down a dark path. We both know what it's like to have a parent who works too hard. And neither of us had the chance to ask them to slow down and just be there for us."

"I don't want Charlie to grow up without a mother at home. He's already got divorced parents." Mascara smeared across my cheeks.

"You have a rare opportunity, though—one our fathers never had."

"What's that?"

"You have a chance to change."

William pulled me up and held me closely. I nuzzled into his shoulder and cried until no more tears escaped from my ducts. His warm body against mine reassured me I wasn't alone and someone was there to catch me when I fell. I promised myself, from here on out, my first and main priority would always be my son. The work would always be there, but my son wouldn't always be a child. I needed to break the cycle, and I needed to do it right now.

Chapter Twenty-Eight

AMELIA

"Thank you for understanding, Ross. I know I'm still new here, and I want to make a good impression, but this is the right thing for me right now."

"No further explanation needed. We want our employees to be happy and healthy. You deserve a vacation."

"Will someone else be able to handle Leo's case? I have all the files together on my desk. Karen could provide them to the new assigned attorney."

"Yes, absolutely. Don't even worry about it!"

Ross and I shook hands, and I promised to be back in two weeks with a clear mind and a more regulated schedule. Even my boss noticed I put in far too much time at the office and exceeded all billable hour requirements. I promised myself and Charlie I would only work late if it was an emergency.

For the next week and a half, Charlie and I spent our time together all day and all night. I told him soon enough he'd get sick of me, but he said it wasn't possible.

I planned a ton of great adventures for us during our mini vacation. Of course, his teachers weren't too thrilled I was pulling him out of school for two weeks, but I told them it couldn't be avoided. I didn't tell them we were going to an amusement park, a water park and then to his father's wedding. I imagined they'd frown upon most of those excuses.

"Mom, can William come with us to the parks?"

"I don't think so, sweetie. He still has to work."

"Is he still coming to the wedding?"

"Absolutely."

Charlie high-fived me and galloped to his room to finish packing. I needed to pack, too. As I folded clean laundry in the living room, someone knocked at the front door. I set down the beach towel in my hands and strode over to welcome my unexpected guest.

"William!" I cried when I opened the door.

He strutted inside with a new pair of Levis on his hips and a black tee shirt hugging his chest. Since moving into the halfway house, and now having a steady paycheck, William could afford to eat regularly and even go to the gym. He shed his lean, almost meek appearance, and added a sufficient amount of muscle to his arms, legs and abdomen. That and his beard stirred up feelings deep inside my belly I hadn't felt in quite some time.

"Hey. Just wanted to stop by before you left." He handed me a paper bag, of which I already knew its origin.

I opened the treat and inside stood a red velvet cupcake from my favorite bakery in the city. "That's so sweet of you."

He pulled me into his arms, and I absorbed the sweet, clean aroma of his cologne. The first time I met William, he could barely stand to be near me. Now? We hugged hello and goodbye almost every time we saw each other. My little "breakdown" seemed to knock down another part of the walls around his heart. I felt closer to him than ever, and I missed him dearly when we weren't together. Again, the idea of having a romantic relationship with William nudged my conscience. We'd both come so far from when we met. Could we fit into each other's lives as more than friends?

"William!" Charlie pounded across the hardwood floor and leapt into William's arms. "I wish you were coming with us."

"Me too! But you and your mom are going to have a great time. Then, before you know it, I'll be there for the wedding."

Charlie hugged William tightly, and my heart nearly burst at its seams. They'd grown quite close since they met unexpectedly all those weeks ago. The doubts I once had about bringing William around Charlie vanished a while back. I trusted William with my son more than nearly anyone else in our lives. I still couldn't thank him enough for supporting Charlie the night of his play, when I wasn't there. Sure, it hurt to know someone else had to do it in my absence, but I'm relieved it was William.

"You're good with a ride to the ceremony?"

"Yeah, not a problem. A friend from work is driving me there. He has family in Pittsburgh, so he figured it'd give him a reason to go and visit."

"Perfect, I'm glad it worked out. Then, you'll be able to cruise with us on the way home."

William set Charlie down and pulled something from his back pocket. "This is for you, Charlie."

Sparkles in Charlie's eyes illuminated his face as he greedily grabbed for the envelope.

"What do you say, Charlie?"

"Sorry. Thank you!"

He tore open the envelope, and inside was a crisp twenty dollar bill. "So you can get a souvenir at one of the parks."

"Wow!" Charlie gazed at the bill in his hand as though Benjamin Franklin stared back at him instead of Andrew Jackson.

"It's not much," William whispered bashfully.

"It's incredibly generous. Thank you."

William hugged us each again one more time before he left and Charlie's and my vacation began.

Chapter Twenty-Nine

AMELIA

Charlie and I, exhausted yet fulfilled, left the water park and drove to our hometown. Even though I still carried the guilt of missing Charlie's play, I think I helped make up for it on our little trip. Watching Charlie fearlessly dive down waterslides and holler at the top of roller coasters reassured me that a vacation together was exactly what we needed.

Driving down the all-too-familiar highways sent a shiver or two down my spine. I didn't think I'd be back "home" so soon, and yet here I was, only a half hour away from the hotel where my ex-husband planned to marry a new woman.

We arrived at the hotel around two, which left us enough time to check in, get dressed and head down to one of the banquet halls in the hotel for the ceremony. William arrived not too long after we did and joined us in our shared hotel room to dress for the ceremony. Charlie was the ring bearer, and I couldn't wait to see him walk down the aisle.

Naturally, Cal chose the ritziest hotel in Candlebrook. Money wasn't the issue; I could afford it but didn't know why he had to have something so ostentatious. Did he forget he already got married once? And let me tell you, we spared no expense for our wedding day.

Chandeliers hung every several feet in the hallway, and the walls were lined with pristine artwork.

"I'm not sure if I belong in this kind of place," William joked.

"Me either."

"This place is cool! Like a castle!" Charlie shouted. I shushed him as we found our room.

I tapped the key against the door as it magically unlocked. Back in my day, we had to insert the key; now you just needed it to touch the door.

The room housed two king-sized beds, a balcony, a refrigerator, a maroon suede loveseat and more. The curtains were made of lace, and the plush navy carpet squeezed between my toes. If you searched for luxury in the dictionary, this hotel room would be smack dab next to the definition.

Charlie dropped his backpack and dove head first onto the cream down comforter. "Mom, check this out!" He jumped on the bed and managed an awe-inspiring flip.

"Charlie!" I rebuked. Then William hopped onto the bed and jumped alongside Charlie.

"You two are too much." I couldn't help but smile, though. Their laughter echoed within the room, and I grinned ear to ear.

"C'mon, Mom. Join us!" Charlie called out.

Against my better judgment, I joined my two favorite guys, jumping as high as I could, almost touching the ceiling.

"William, will you zip me up?"

I stood in the vanity mirror with my lilac floor-length gown glittering in my reflection. My hair hung in soft, wavy tendrils while my shimmering nude eyeshadow sparkled under the lights. I spritzed a touch of Chanel perfume on the nape of my neck and applied a smooth coat of lipstick. I felt like a princess, and judging by William's expression, I looked like one, too.

"Wow, Amelia," he gasped. "You look gorgeous."

I blushed. "Thanks."

Carefully, William caressed the small of my back as he lightly grasped the zipper and pulled it up to my neckline. He put his arms around me and rested his head on my shoulder. We gazed at each other through our reflection, and happiness radiated off both our illuminated faces.

"I'm really happy you're here," I said.

"Me, too. Although you're going to piss Cal off, you know?"

I raised my eyebrows. "As opposed to any other time I see him?"

"Well, what's he going to do when his ex-wife shows up his

bride on their wedding day? There's no way she'll even compare to you today."

Damn, this man had stolen my heart, and I don't think I'll ever get it back.

"Are you guys going to get married too?" Charlie chirped up.

William choked on the water he sipped from the bottle on the dresser, and I burst into laughter.

"You're something else, kid." I said.

"Mom, do I have to dance with any girls later?"

I snickered. "Not if you don't want to."

"Good. But if I change my mind, am I allowed?"

"Sure, sweetie."

My iPhone alarm rang, signaling it was time for us to head down to the ceremony.

"Charlie, I'll walk you to where you should be, but then William and I are going to take our seats. Okay?"

"Sure, Mom."

Together, all three of us left the hotel room, me in my dress, William and Charlie in their suits, and took the elevator to the ground floor where the ceremony and reception would be held. It amazed me suits small enough to fit Charlie even existed. He looked like my little knight in shining cotton.

Guests poured in as I waved to some I knew. Out of the corner of my eye, I saw Cal's parents, and my stomach dropped. I hadn't seen them since before our divorce. They weren't fond of my decision to move Charlie a few hundred miles away, and so the sour looks on their faces didn't surprise me.

"Grace, Jeffrey," I said as they approached us.

Grace sized me up, her eyes trailing up and down my body several times. I felt like a piece of cattle about to be auctioned off.

"It's been a while," she responded airily.

"Uh huh."

"Ready, kiddo?" Jeffrey asked Charlie.

"As I'll ever be!"

Charlie's grandparents smiled, and while I wasn't thrilled to see them, it was nice to see they still loved Charlie so much despite my differences with their son.

"Good luck, Charlie! I'll see you soon." I bent down and pulled him into my arms. I feared he might protest, but instead, he hugged me back.

"You look so pretty, Mama."

"I love you, sweetheart."

I let go, and Charlie skipped away with his grandfather toward the room where I assumed the wedding party planned to gather.

"No introduction?" William teased as we found a pair of seats toward the back of the room where the ceremony was being held.

"Believe me, you don't want to meet my ex-parents-in-law. They're brutal."

"I could tell."

William grasped my hand, and I stifled a gasp. As our fingers interlocked, nervous jitters tittered about in my mind and in my heart, which skipped a beat when I looked over to him. Something magical had bloomed between us; I could feel it in my bones.

I put my head on William's shoulder and closed my eyes. How did I get so lucky to have him by my side? William had grown to be my rock and my shoulder to lean on. I never felt a connection this intensely before, not even with the man standing at the altar a few feet away from me.

Ethereal music crooned from the speakers as William and I turned around to see the wedding party walk down the aisle. Angela's sister, the Maid of Honor, stepped cautiously down the aisle first. She linked arms with Cal's best friend, Tony. Tony smiled brightly at me, and I winked back. Cal kept Tony in the divorce, but we still talked on Facebook from time to time. He was a good man, and I couldn't for the life of me understand how he put up with Cal for so many years.

A few more bridesmaids and groomsmen strolled down the

red carpeted walkway, then Charlie appeared arm and arm with the flower girl, Angela's niece. She tossed rose petals along the carpet, and Charlie offered his brilliant smile to the guests. A single tear fell down my cheek as Charlie waved to William and me. I wished I could have hugged him right then and there. My boy looked so grown up and handsome.

William squeezed my hand. Knowing my son and William were with me was the best thing I could have ever asked for. At long last, the guests rose as Angela and her father ambled down the aisle. She looked beautiful; I couldn't deny that. I said a silent prayer in my mind for the girl. I did not envy her, but I wished her the best. Cal and I were never meant for each other. Maybe she'd have better luck.

I focused my attention on Charlie while he swayed side to side standing next to his father. His movements were either the result of extreme nerves or the fact he hadn't gone to the bathroom before walking down the aisle. I tried not to giggle, and William smiled too.

"Do you, Calvin, take Angela to be your lawfully wedded wife, in sickness and in health, for richer or for poorer, for as long as you both shall live?"

"I do."

"And, do you, Angela, take Calvin to be your lawfully wedded husband, in sickness and in health, for richer or for poorer, for as long as you both shall live?"

"I do!"

"Then, it is my honor and duty to announce, Calvin, that you may kiss your bride!"

Cal pulled Angela into a close embrace and kissed her passionately. I pushed the memory of my own wedding day and wedding kiss from my mind. I wonder if people thought we'd last after we walked out of the church. Finally, they stopped kissing, and the people on both sides of the room stood and erupted with cheers and laughter.

Charlie ran into my arms once I found him in the decadent ballroom where the reception was being held. I squeezed him tightly and congratulated him on a job well done as ring bearer.

"Woohoo!" Charlie sprinted off to play with the other kids, and I gulped down the rest of my drink.

William and I found our seats located at the table with a few other couples I'd never met. Soon, we discovered they worked with Angela at the restaurant where she still tended bar. They seemed friendly enough, but it didn't matter; I had the best date in the whole damn room.

A large, glittering, crystal chandelier hung from the center of the room, and all the tables were lined with rose satin tablecloths. In the center of each of the twenty or so tables stood a dozen white roses in genuine crystal vases. A quartet played in the corner while waiters dressed better than some of the guests offered drinks and hors d'oeuvres to those mingling. Every detail down to the silverware was epically perfect. If I had to guess, even Prince William and Kate would have been a little jealous of this reception.

Charlie sat with the rest of the wedding party. It felt selfish, but I wanted my boy by my side instead of watching Cal's family smother him. I wondered if I'd ever stop feeling as protective as a mama bear around Cal and his family. Maybe someday.

The quartet slowed their pace as the servers brought out the first course: a garden salad with the greenest, freshest vegetables I'd ever seen. By now, the vodka from my second martini walloped me. I needed something to soak it up. The salad and rolls, also at the table, would have to do until the main course arrived.

"Feeling okay?" William asked thoughtfully. "I want to be able to show you my moves later!"

"You have moves?" I raised an eyebrow.

"Not very good ones, but I have 'em." His smile could have lit up the entire city.

William reached under the table and massaged my bare knee.

His fingers moved in a circular motion, and the tingles danced all the way up my legs and into my belly. Suddenly, I didn't care about the future; I only cared about this exact moment. I wanted his lips against mine and much, much more.

A server delivered my perfectly cut piece of steak shortly after the salads arrived, and my mouth watered immediately. William ordered the same, and we smiled at each other as we dug in like children on Christmas morning as they open presents.

I stifled a moan as I chewed the savory steak. The couples at the table eyed me disapprovingly, but it wasn't every day you had the best piece of filet mignon in your life! With steak still in my mouth, I smiled and gave them the thumbs up. They avoided talking to William and me for the rest of dinner. They seemed stuck up, anyway. William and I made our own fun as we finished our meals and people-watched.

"I bet that guy is going to hit on one of the bridesmaids," he predicted.

"How do you know?"

"He hasn't stopped staring at her all night, and I can tell by the look on his face."

"Oh yeah?"

"Yeah, it's how I look at you."

I blushed, and without thinking, without worry if I was making a mistake, I lightly kissed him on the lips. Who would have known, the man I met, who lived on the streets, would one day turn into the man I couldn't stop thinking about? Life was funny like that. Sometimes the greatest moments happened when we least expected it.

Once the plates were cleared and toasts finished, the DJ picked up the pace and urged guests to hit the dance floor. William didn't waste any time dragging me out to the center of the ballroom to show me his "moves."

We spent the next two hours dancing, laughing, sweating, and falling even more deeply for each other than we ever thought possible.

Chapter Thirty-One

AMELIA

William, Charlie and I were some of the last guests to leave the ballroom. Surprisingly, Charlie didn't slow down and out-danced even me! The kid had stamina, what could I say? Although it could have been the extra slice of cake I watched him sneak from another table. The mom in me wanted to scold him, but it was far too funny to watch as he looked behind both shoulders before he took the piece and devoured it within seconds.

William showed me his dance moves, which were far better than I pictured. Mostly, he made me laugh until I felt a new pair of abs shredding through. The most surprising event of the night, however, was when Cal asked to cut in and dance with me. I almost told him "no thanks" but decided to try and keep the peace instead.

"Are you having fun?" he asked shyly.

"You sure know how to throw a party. Have you done this before?" I teased.

"Ouch."

We both smiled.

"It's been a long time since we danced together," I said.

"Sure has. Hey, listen, Amelia—"

"Yeah?"

William eyed us from the table, and I noticed a hint of jealousy in his serious glare. Would it make me a bad person if I liked seeing him a little jealous?

"I just want to say thank you for everything you're doing for Charlie. He seems to be happy at his new school."

"Well, it *is* my job."

"I know, but you're an amazing mom, and he's lucky to have someone who cares for him so deeply."

"Thanks, Cal. You're an okay dad, too. But you may want to tone down the 'tude around him, okay? He's starting to sound like a mini-you."

"You kiddin' me? His fire is all you!"

I rolled my eyes.

"We raised a pretty good kid, huh?" Cal asked.

We both glanced over to see Charlie slow-dancing with the flower girl. Even though I secretly knew my son was terrified of catching cooties from a girl, it was beyond adorable to see him with his hands on her hips and a broad smile spread across his face.

"We sure did."

Silence took over the conversation as we swayed awkwardly to the music.

"So, I wanted to tell you something."

"Oh, boy. Here we go."

"Angela is pregnant."

"Already?"

Cal blushed, and I honestly can't remember a time I saw such a blissful look on his face. Maybe when I told him *I* was pregnant all those years ago.

"I'm very happy for you," I said evenly.

"I just wanted to let you know before I told Charlie."

"Thank you. I appreciate it."

"So, what's going on with you and that guy?" He asked casually, but I sensed a sourness in his tone.

"His name is William." I rolled my eyes.

"Yeah, him." Cal smiled, and I realized he enjoyed taunting me. What a surprise.

"He makes me happy," I admitted.

"Treating you well?"

"Very. We're good together."

Cal ignored my jab. "Is he good with Charlie?"

"Treats him like a son."

Cal winced. "Well, that's good."

William strode over to us as the song was winding down. "May I cut back in?"

Cal breathed a sigh of relief. "Sure, man."

My ex-husband squeezed my hand, and with a quick smile, he walked back over to his blushing bride, who waved to me. I waved back. Angela wasn't so bad, and she did make a damn gorgeous bride.

"What was that all about?" William asked.

"Just a friendly chat among ex-partners." I laughed.

William shook his head and spun me around as a new pop hit blasted from the speakers.

By the end of the night, I had to drag Charlie off the dance floor and back to our room. Charlie and I slept in one of the beds while William took ownership of the other. Before we drifted off to sleep, though, William kissed us both goodnight. I fell fast asleep as soon as my head hit the pillow and slept better than I had in a very long time.

———

Cal and Angela invited us all to join them for a family breakfast the following day. I declined. Even though it turned out to be a beautiful wedding, one night with my ex and his new wife was enough for me.

Reluctantly, William, Charlie and I packed our bags and checked out of the beautiful hotel. I didn't want to leave, but I also couldn't wait to go home. William offered to drive the way back, for which I felt eternally grateful. I may have had one too many glasses of champagne after dinner, and my head throbbed painfully.

The drive home seemed longer than the drive to the hotel, which made me all the more anxious to be home. About halfway through our drive, we stopped for gas and a quick bite to eat. Charlie and I stood in line for pizza while William waited in the Mexican line. If only all gas stations were as fancy as this one, I thought.

Charlie rehashed the previous night and how fun it'd been to dance with Hallie, the flower girl. He blushed when I asked if he had a crush on her.

"No way, Mom! That's gross!"

I ruffled his hair and smiled.

A phone rang loudly and echoed throughout the eating area. I turned to see William answer the call, his face as white as a ghost. My stomach dropped as William's eyes grew, and he used his free hand to touch his forehead in distress. I wanted to go over to him to see what was the matter, but I also didn't want to leave Charlie in line by himself.

I anxiously waited to catch William's attention as tears streamed down his face.

Screw it.

I grasped Charlie's hand, and we exited the line.

"What's wrong with William, Mommy?"

"I don't know, sweetie."

William turned to see us walking swiftly toward him, and he shook his head. Tears glistened in his eyes, and I couldn't imagine who could be on the other end of the phone call.

Charlie tugged on my coat. "Hold on, Charlie."

We stood awkwardly in the middle of the gas station while William crumbled into a chair. I gave Charlie a wrinkled twenty dollar bill from my purse, instructing him to go pick out a handful of snacks for the ride home and to hurry.

William ended the phone call and sat with his head in his hands. Tension mounted as I lightly put my hand on his shoulder. He jumped at my touch.

"What's going on?"

"We have to go. I can't be here."

"Tell me, what is it?"

"I can't talk about it right now. We have to go."

He strode out of the gas station and jumped into the driver's seat of my car. My heart ached for him. I'd never seen him so distressed or shaken up. I collected Charlie from the register, and we returned to the car as well.

We drove in silence the rest of the way back home, but the lack of conversation was deafening. Even Charlie knew something was wrong and stared out of the window quietly. He didn't even play his game. All the horrible scenarios ran through my head during the ride. Did someone die? Did someone he knows get hurt? Was there an accident at the halfway house? My heart thudded in my chest. I reached to touch his hand with mine, but he pulled away. His desire not to be touched stung. I wanted to be there for him, to comfort him as he'd done for me during my dark time.

William parked the car outside the halfway house, grabbed his bags and headed toward the building. He didn't say goodbye. Charlie and I looked to each other in confusion.

"Is William okay, Mama?"

"I don't know."

I realized this was one of those times I needed to give William his space despite the desperation in my soul to go to him and help him through whatever'd just happened.

Charlie and I arrived home, less than thrilled to be here. Our vacation was over and devastation awaited our arrival. I couldn't stop thinking about William and the haunted expression he bore after answering the phone.

I swallowed forcefully and dialed his number.

"William?"

Sobs echoed through the phone.

"What's wrong? Are you okay? Talk to me!"

"He's dead! He's dead! Oh my, God, he's dead!" he lamented.

I wasn't sure who he referred to, but the sound of William's shattered heart erupting through the phone was breaking mine.

As I opened my mouth to ask who passed away, the dial tone pinged in my ear.

Chapter Thirty-Two

AMELIA

"Mom? Is William okay?"

"I don't think so."

"What can we do to help him?"

"I don't know, bud. Something really bad happened."

"I don't want him to be sad."

"Me, either sweetie. Would you mind if I called Carrie to come over and watch you? I want to check in on William."

"Why can't I come?" Charlie pouted.

Truth be told, I knew William still harbored the demons inside his soul. No one can shed the damage he'd had very easily. I didn't want Charlie to be exposed to whatever hurt William so badly. I wanted to help William, but I also needed to protect my son.

"I think it's an adult problem."

"But I'm a big kid!"

"I know you are, but not this time. Okay? I need you to be strong and brave for me. Be good for Carrie, too."

Carrie arrived a half hour later with movies and pizza in tow for her and Charlie.

"Thank you so much. I'm sorry for the last minute notice."

"All good, Ms. Montgomery."

I kissed my son goodbye and couldn't help but sprint to my car. I sped to the halfway house and parked as close as I could to the building. I knocked repeatedly on the door until someone opened it and let me in. It wasn't the manager, but another resident. I smiled briefly and tore through the house to William's room.

Inside, William rocked back and forth, hugging his knees. Tears poured down his crestfallen face. His eyes, swollen and red, appeared empty and desolate.

On one wall of the room hung a beautifully sewn American flag. On another, there were a few family portraits of him with his parents. In the corner of the room, I spotted a picture of Charlie and me. William must have taken it from my apartment when I wasn't looking. My heart ached for him.

"Talk to me, babe. What's going on?"

"Hudson. Hudson's dead."

I rubbed his back and waited for him to elaborate. I'd never heard him mention a Hudson before. I didn't know if it was his brother, friend, or someone else entirely.

"We served together," he said, noticing my confusion.

I nodded as it all began to make sense. A fresh wave of grief washed over William as he sobbed again. I was at a loss about what to do. I'd never seen him, let alone any man, so upset in my entire life.

"I'm so sorry, William. I'm so sorry," I uttered in his ear.

"Hudson was one of two of my best friends in the service. We had basic training together and ended up overseas together, too. We went through everything together. We kept each other sane— even when our other buddy, Spence, died. We were like brothers."

I nodded and encouraged him to keep going. I wondered if talking about it would help ease his pain.

"I never told you this, but when Spence died in combat, I couldn't handle it. Even with Hudson still by my side, I lost it.

When my tour ended, and I was up for re-enlistment, I decided not to go back. I couldn't do it. There were other reasons I didn't go back, too, but I abandoned my brother. I couldn't handle the death of our other brother, Spence. I feel like a disgrace to my country and Hudson. I wasn't there for him when he needed me most. I abandoned him."

William shook as his emotions took hold once again. I put my arms around him and prayed that my touch and love would soothe him, but then again, I wasn't sure anything would make William feel better at this moment.

"I wasn't there for my father when he died; I wasn't there for Spence and now Hudson. I'm a failure, and I'm weak."

William broke free of my grasp, pulling away. Truly at a loss for words, my heart broke for the man I realized I loved so damn much. Out of nowhere, William howled in agony and punched the wall. I gasped, my eyes growing scared and shocked. William slumped against the hole he'd manufactured and held his stomach while he doubled over. His hand bled freely, blood dripping to the floor.

"I'm a loser," he repeated over and over. "I don't deserve to be alive. I should have died in Afghanistan. I should die now!"

"No, you're not! Stop saying that! You're a brave man, William."

He looked up at me with bloodshot eyes and a broken heart. His face pleaded for peace of mind, which I couldn't give to him. There was nothing I could say to make him feel better. Nothing in the entire world.

After losing my father, my mother, my two best friends, and my home, I didn't think I had anything left to lose. The reality of losing Hudson hit me like a moving train. Or like someone cut out a piece of my heart and shoved it down a garbage disposal.

Emptiness erupted in my soul, and my body crumbled beneath its metaphorical weight. I couldn't see my future, and I didn't want to. I didn't feel I had any right to continue living. Why did I deserve another chance at life when so many people I cared about weren't afforded the same opportunity? What made me so special? Why was I special?

Amelia left after a few hours to go home and check on Charlie. I didn't blame her; I wouldn't want to stick around to see me sink below the depths of reality, either. Before she left, she wrapped her arms around my neck and kissed my forehead. But I didn't feel it. My body rejected her warmth and kindness. I wanted her to leave. I wanted to be alone.

Once she closed the door, my demons took hold. I turned off all the lights in my room and lay on my bed, motionless. The sunset and the moon had risen by now, just as the light had left my life, surrounding me in darkness too.

Sleep wouldn't come either. My mind wandered and dragged me into the past, farther back than I ever wanted to go.

I was on the streets again, lost and wandering down the avenues bursting with people who have their lives together. I was just another face in a crowd of humans. No one noticed me, and I didn't notice them. There I was, back in the desert, with my two friends beside me. One was blown away, never to exist again. Even farther back, I stood watching as the towers burned from the inside out. Smoke and ash filled the air, and I knew my father was gone. He was dead. They were all dead.

I don't know how long I lay there, unmoving, but the sun rose once again. But I couldn't bring myself to do the same. It was Monday, and I had to go to work, but I couldn't imagine leaving my room. I couldn't imagine pretending like everything is okay.

For the first time in several hours, I managed to hoist myself off my bed and reach for my burner phone. It was all I could afford with my first paycheck after paying rent and buying groceries. I called my boss and let him know I was sick and wouldn't make it in today. Guilt weighed heavily on my stomach. I couldn't afford to miss a day of work, and yet I couldn't afford to be at work either.

I knew what I needed to do: shower, eat breakfast, and brush my teeth. I knew I should call Hudson's parents and tell them how sorry I am for the loss of their son. I should call his wife and my goddaughter. I should be there to support all the others affected by his death. But, I couldn't. I really couldn't. I knew it was selfish. I knew his wife was suffering, and his daughter would grow up without a father. I knew I was a bastard for only caring about myself, but it didn't stop me from doing it.

Amelia called me four times and texted during the night. I hadn't replied and didn't want to either. I didn't want to talk to anybody, because the only voice I wanted to hear was that of a man on a flight back to the United States, in a casket wrapped with a flag. Hudson was the only person I wanted, and he was the one I could't have.

I should have been in the casket, not him. He has a family and a future. Well, had.

Eventually, I drifted in and out of restless sleep. Helicopters and gunshots rattled my mind. There was another war; only this time, it was inside me.

I spent the next three days in the same routine. Tossing and turning in my bed, avoiding all phone calls except to call in sick, and missing the fuck out of everyone in my life who left too soon.

Amelia stopped by last night, but I pretended to be asleep. She knocked a few times and struggled to open the door. I locked it for this exact purpose. I didn't want her pity or her sympathy. I deserved to suffer, and I deserved to be all alone. Not to mention, she didn't deserve a man in her life who'd drag her down into his pit of misery. Amelia was a good woman with a big heart. She could do better than me.

Thursday arrived, and I still hadn't eaten, bathed or gone to work. Someone knocked firmly on my bedroom door, but I didn't move to answer it.

"William?" The halfway house's manager called. "I'm sorry, but I need you to open the door. I've gotten several calls about you, and I need to see you. It's after seven o'clock at night; open up!"

I sighed and realized I couldn't hide any longer. I slid out of bed, avoiding the reflection in the mirror as I unlocked the door.

The manager stepped in, and his jaw dropped. "William!" he gasped. "Are you okay? Do you need a doctor?"

White spots invaded my vision, and the room spun rapidly around me. My manager's voice faded, and within seconds everything went dark.

Chapter Thirty-Four

AMELIA

An ambulance arrived at the halfway house. The manager called me as soon as William fainted on his bedroom floor. I wanted to drive to see him, but the manager advised it'd be better to meet the paramedics at the hospital. I didn't have time to call a sitter for Charlie, so we grabbed our coats and sprinted to my car.

"Is he okay?" Charlie asked frantically while I parked in the Emergency Room lot.

"He will be, sweetheart. He's just handling some difficult stuff. Difficult things affect people differently. Everyone handles bad news in a different way."

Charlie and I jogged inside the hospital and searched for the Emergency Room. I stopped a doctor sauntering down the hallway with a few clipboards in tow.

"Excuse me, doctor? Can you please point me to the Emergency Room? My boyfriend is here, and I need to find him."

"Sure, Miss. It's down the hall and to your right. You can't miss it."

"Thanks!"

Charlie held my hand as we speed-walked in the direction the doctor pointed. The familiar sterile hospital smell wafted through my nose as other medical staff scurried around as though someone had cut their heads off.

"Mom?"

"Yes?"

"Is William your boyfriend?"

"What makes you think that?"

"Uh, because you told the doctor your boyfriend was here."

Did I say that? Really? I didn't even realize I called William my boyfriend just then.

"I didn't mean to say that," I said, gasping for breath.

We approached the ER reception desk, and an annoyed-looking nurse typed madly on her keyboard.

"Hello?" I tried to grab her attention. "I'm here to see William Divola."

"Sorry," she screeched. "Only immediate family members allowed." She didn't look away from her computer for a second.

"He doesn't have any immediate family. His parents are deceased, and he's an only child. I'm all he has right now. Can I please see him?"

The red-headed nurse, who appeared to be around sixty, eyed me suspiciously. "Let me call back and check to see if it's okay with the patient."

"Thank you so much. I appreciate it."

The nurse, whose name tag read "Nancy," picked up the phone and asked a nurse if William approved of my visit. Much to her dismay, Nancy nodded toward the door leading to ER patients and away from reception. I imagined she wasn't a fan of breaking the rules. Usually, I wasn't either.

I didn't wait around for her to change her mind as I pulled Charlie through the heavy swinging doors. As soon as we stepped foot in the actual ER, Charlie and I covered our ears as a young child screamed at the top of her lungs. It broke my heart and my eardrums at the same time. A nurse looked at me and mouthed,

"Broken ankle." I nodded and craned my neck, looking for William.

Out of the corner of my eye, I saw William in a bed with an oxygen mask firmly secured to his face.

"William!" Charlie shouted.

Charlie sprinted over to William, almost knocking down a nurse carrying a tray covered in medical supplies. The woman smiled and walked toward another patient. I gave her an apologetic smile and followed him to William's bed.

Charlie dove onto William's belly and hugged him. "I'm glad you're okay. You scared us."

William held Charlie in his embrace. "I'm sorry for worrying you, Charlie."

"Bud, why don't you head back to the waiting room? I'd like a minute with William."

"Do I have to?" Charline whined.

"Yes, please. It will only be a few minutes."

The nurse from a few moments ago overheard the conversation and offered to walk Charlie back to the waiting room. Once Charlie was out of earshot, I pulled up a chair and held William's hand in my own.

"Are you okay?" I breathed heavily.

William's eyes, bloodshot and hollow, bore into mine. With just a look, I felt his sadness inside my own heart.

"I don't really know."

"What happened?"

"I guess I passed out. Doc said low blood sugar. I didn't eat much the past few days."

"Oh, William." I laid my head on his arm with the ER bracelet and closed my eyes. I would do anything to take away his pain. I'd even absorb it if I could. "I'm here for you."

"I know. Thank you."

"I talked to your manager at work—"

William's eyes bulged outside his head.

"Don't worry! I didn't give any specific details, but I told him you had a medical emergency. He said to take as much time as you need. Your job will be waiting for you when you are healthy again."

"He said that?"

"Told you it was a great place to work!"

"What would I do without you, Amelia?"

Carefully, I stood and leaned in closer to the man to whom my heart felt magnetized. As gently as I could, I placed my lips against his and rested my forehead against his own.

"Everything is going to be okay. We're in this together."

———

Doctors released William later that day once his vitals returned to normal and his body had the chance to rehydrate. The doctor and psychiatrist at the hospital spent a great deal of time with William before they discharged him, though. They believed he suffered from severe PTSD and that treatment would be necessary to help him recover from the traumatic experiences in his life. William assumed he was handling everything fine, but after speaking with the psychiatrist, he agreed he hadn't done much to manage the loss and devastation he faced in the past decade or so.

"I'm afraid the meds will bum me out or turn my brain into mush," he said as we pulled away from the hospital.

"You'll never know until you try. Plus, if you don't like it, there's always something else the doctors can try."

That night, William took his anti-anxiety pills before we put Charlie to bed and picked out a movie to watch on Netflix at my apartment. I wanted him to spend the night. I didn't want him to be alone.

We argued for a few minutes while I scanned through the choices, but we settled on a rom-com movie. I wanted him to relax, not get hyped up over the latest and greatest action flick.

"Are you sure you want to watch this?" he pleaded.

"The reviews were great!"

William huffed as I put my head on his shoulder and grasped his hand in mine.

"I'm glad you're okay," I said. "I don't know what I would have done if something happened to you." The thought of something more serious needled its way into my mind and felt like a left hook to my heart.

"Me, too." He rubbed my back gently.

"How do you feel so far? Feel any different?"

"I feel the same, but maybe a touch calmer."

"That's great," I urged.

I leaned in closer and kissed his lips. "How about now?"

"Even better."

Deep down, I knew I should give William time to recover from the stress of mourning his friend, but I also wanted to make him feel better. Not to mention, I felt closer to him than ever, and I wanted to *show* him just how much he meant to me.

Our next kiss ignited something inside my soul. My belly flip-flopped to the thud of my racing heart. Our tongues found each other, and passion exploded throughout every cell in my body. He pulled me onto his lap, and the friction between us could have created a series of sparks in the air.

"It's been a really long time," he said with a husky, desperate tone.

"Me, too. Are you sure this is okay?"

"It's more than okay. It's perfect."

He peeled my top off and tossed it aside. My golden honey hair covered my breasts, but William moved the tendrils aside. "You're so beautiful." He delicately kissed my neck, and I pulled his shirt off while I struggled to catch my breath.

William picked me up and gently set me down on the couch before climbing on top of me. His dog tags clung to his chest, already covered in sweat. He was my life-sized G.I. Joe, and I wanted to see him in action. He unzipped my jeans, pulling them off with ease. He kissed my neck all the way down to belly, then traveled even further south.

I stifled my moans as ecstasy mounted deep within my core. His hands discovered me as I explored his body too. His newly formed muscles rippled through his skin, and my jaw dropped as he took off his sweatpants, revealing a mouthwatering "V" pointing exactly where I wanted to go.

William smiled and removed the last of my clothing with delight. I took a deep breath as the man I'd fallen hopelessly in love with made love to me.

———

William and I woke as the sunshine sprawled through my window. I yawned and stretched, then turned over to see William staring at me with a goofy grin.

"Morning!"

"It's a good morning when I wake up next to you." He kissed my forehead and pulled me into a loving embrace.

As I lay with William's arms wrapped around me, one particular feeling came to mind: safety. Even though I could handle myself in a courtroom and take care of my son, I couldn't describe the happiness which ebbed and flowed throughout my body. I finally felt safe in another man's arms. William changed the way I saw and thought about men. He proved men could be sensitive and brave. He showed me a man could take care of me the way I needed to be while loving my son as his own, too.

As I reveled in the feeling of having my love next to me, my other love, much smaller, created a racket from his room.

"Charlie's awake," I murmured.

I rose out of bed and pulled on my zebra pattern fleece robe. William raised an eyebrow, and I stuck out my tongue.

"It's comfortable!" I whispered.

William snickered, shook his head and followed me out of the bedroom.

"William!" Charlie cried from the living room. "You're still here!"

"Of course I am, kiddo. What'cha want for breakfast?"

"What do you mean? Like cereal?"

"No, I'm going to cook breakfast for us."

"Really? Mom never cooks us breakfast."

I blushed. It was true, though. I rarely had time to make Charlie's lunch in the morning, let alone throw together breakfast.

"How about an omelet?"

"What's that?" Charlie asked curiously.

"It's the breakfast of superheroes!"

Charlie's eyes lit up as he jumped up and down. "Yes! I want an omelet!"

I eyed my son carefully.

"Please?" he corrected himself.

I nodded with approval.

"Coming right up!" William promised.

While Charlie played his XBox, I sat bemused as William whipped up a fantastic breakfast. He made each of us a veggie omelet with wheat toast and orange juice on the side. My mouth watered as the aroma of sautéed vegetables and cheese wafted into the air. I paused to absorb the scene before me and wondered if this is what my life would be like going forward: Charlie playing, William cooking, and all of us together as a family.

My heart burst with love, which also terrified me. If there was one thing I've learned in life, it's that when you have something to love, you also have something to lose. I shook away any negative thoughts as William whistled to Charlie and brought the plates full of steaming food to the table.

After breakfast, William offered to do the dishes, and at that moment I considered bending down on my damn knee and asking him to marry me. Where did this guy come from? Mars, I suspected. I cleaned up the apartment a little while Charlie busied himself in his room with a science project for school. Luckily, Charlie enjoyed those kinds of assignments, and it rarely turned into the kind of project which required me to finish it or do it myself.

"What do you think you want to do today?" I asked William. "Charlie is off from school."

He looked down at his feet shyly. "I think I want to take a run or something. You know, clear my head?"

"Sounds like a great idea!"

William kissed me goodbye, and as soon as the door closed behind him, a tinge of emptiness crept in. I'd never been one to weep over a boy or pine for one either, but William was different. His absence filled the room, and the second he stepped out of view, a pang of loneliness irked me.

"So, Charlie," I said. "What do you want to do today?"

"Mama?"

"Yes, love."

"Can we get a dog?"

I choked on my coffee and took a minute to catch my breath.

"I think we should get a dog," he mused.

"Yeah? And, why's that?"

"To help William. Like a therapy dog."

I opened my mouth to respond but closed it. That wasn't a bad idea, even though I'm sure part of the request stemmed from Charlie's love for animals, especially those of the canine persuasion. I thought about all the medicine the doctors prescribed to William and wondered if a dog might help him even more. I didn't know very much about the process of obtaining a service dog, let alone where we'd go to look for one.

I pulled out my MacBook and set it on the kitchen table.

"Why don't you help me research service dogs? How's that sound?"

"Woohoo!" Charlie chanted as he sped and leaped into my arms.

"Easy there, killer."

After browsing several websites, I came across one which detailed how to obtain a service dog or an emotional support animal. It seemed almost too easy to register a dog as emotional support animal, which was a huge relief. Now, all we needed was the dog.

I called the halfway house manager to explain what I wanted to do for William. At first, I was sure he'd deny the request, but he agreed, saying it sounded like a great idea. A dog would certainly cheer up the other house guests, too.

"All right, kid. Get your sneakers on. We're going to the pound!"

———

Charlie and I drove to the local pet shelter, and my heart shattered as we stepped inside and heard the yelps of all the dogs up for adoption. At least fifty dogs barked and howled in almost-perfect unison.

"There are so many dogs in here, Mom," Charlie whispered.

"I know. It's so sad. I wish we could rescue them all."

"Can we?"

"Not today."

An older woman with gray hair swaying in a long ponytail approached Charlie and me. "Can I help you?" Her smile put me at ease.

"Yes, we're actually in the market to adopt a dog."

"You've come to the right place!" Her honey-brown eyes glowed, and the laugh lines under her eyes appeared more profound up close.

"See, my boyfriend is a veteran and was recently diagnosed with PTSD. I want to get him an emotional support dog to help him with his recovery. Do you think you have any pups who would fit the bill?"

Shawna, as her name tag indicated, bit her cheek and tapped her foot in deep thought. "You know, I think I might have the perfect dog for you!"

She waved us on, and Charlie and I followed closely at her heels. Charlie tugged at my shirt every time we passed a puppy, and I wondered where our dog would be. I loved dogs, but with work and raising a child, I never thought I'd be able to have one. Now seemed like the perfect time if there ever was one.

Shawna stopped at a cubby, and inside, I saw a shy dog whimpering in the corner. "This is Bart," she said proudly. "He's about four years old and was found abandoned on the side of the road two years ago. He's a tad shy, but once he warms up to you, he's the sweetest dog around."

"Do you think he would make a good emotional support dog?" I asked nervously.

"Absolutely. Would you like to meet him?"

I nodded, and Shawna called her assistant to take us to the meet and greet room where she'd bring Bart to us in a few minutes. Charlie and I sat in the designated room where Charlie rocked back in forth with excitement, and I hoped Bart would be just the dog we were looking for.

A few minutes later, as promised, Shawna brought a shy Bart into the playroom. Bart, a golden honey-brown with floppy ears, may have been the cutest mutt I'd ever laid eyes on. As soon as he looked into my eyes, my heart skipped a beat, and I knew he was the one.

"Hi, Bart," I sang. "Come here, buddy."

Bart's tail wagged as his tongue lopped out of his mouth. Shawna nudged him toward us, and much to my surprise, Bart ran to us, then licked Charlie's face. Laughter erupted from the room, and it was clear: we found a pup to bring home to William.

After we left the rescue with a very skittish dog in tow, Charlie and I drove to the pet store to buy Bart food, a bed, a handful of toys, and other canine essentials. With every passing minute, Bart grew a little less frightened and more rambunctious and curious. The pet store near my apartment offered a service dog training session, too. It seemed all the puzzle pieces were falling into place, and for once, fate was on my side.

Bart sported a fancy new camouflage collar and an official service dog tag and vest in case William wanted to take him out of the apartment. I still hadn't figured out who would take care of Bart while William and I were at work, but I was sure we'd figure it out one way or another.

Charlie and I ran a few more errands until the sun set, and my mind wandered and wondered where William could be. I hoped the day proved to be a breath of fresh air, and he found the solace he desperately needed. I also hoped he wouldn't be angry with me that I took it upon myself to adopt an emotional support dog for him.

Although, as I looked at Bart's loving demeanor and puppy

dog face in the rearview mirror, I knew there'd be no way William could be anything less than over the moon.

Once we parked outside the halfway house, I told Charlie he was in charge of Bart, while I carried as much of the supplies as I could hold. Butterflies wrestled in my stomach as we knocked on the front door.

Luckily, William happened to open the door.

"We got you a dog!" Charlie shouted.

Without notice, Bart leapt into William's arms. William's eyes widened, and for a moment, I thought it was fear, but after a second or two, his mouth dropped in awe.

"What's going on?" he asked me, aghast.

"So, um, surprise?" I said shyly.

Bart licked William's face and nuzzled into his neck. He couldn't have weighed more than thirty pounds, and William held him easily in his arms.

"His name is Bart!" Charlie said proudly. "He's your support dog."

"Amelia, is the dog really for me?"

I nodded. William looked from Bart to me and back again. A single tear fell from his cheek, and he snuggled the dog like his child.

"I can't believe this! He's amazing!"

"So, you like him?" I asked as I bit my lip.

"No, I love him! I can't believe you did this for me."

"I'd do anything for you," I whispered in his ear.

William kissed my cheek and set Bart down to explore his new home. He romped around and smelled every square inch of the house. Charlie followed him around, giggling delightedly when Bart licked his face. The other residents peeked around the corner, and smiles soon plastered across their faces too.

"I feel it, Amelia," William said with hope in his voice.

"What's that?"

"Things are going to get better for me, and for us."

"I think so, too." I smiled warmly.

"I think you're right."

"About what?"

"I think maybe, just maybe, I deserve a second chance. I've dwelled so long on the hardships of my life, but I don't want to do that anymore. I want to try and focus on the future. I owe it to those I've lost to give it a try."

As I stared into his eyes, feeling the love emanating from his smile, I knew this was real. *We* could be real. For every night I cried myself to sleep, for every time I thought I'd end up alone, for every day I watched other couples in love, I never thought I'd find happiness again too. All the doubt, worries, and fear were washed away with the coming of a new tide. William was the moon, and I, the ocean, drawn to each other beyond all measure.

———

As the weeks passed, my little family grew tighter than ever. While William kept his room at the halfway house, he stopped by my apartment almost daily. His meds seemed to be working, and he returned to work. He saw a counselor a couple times a week, and I could tell, deep down, his heart was carefully being restored. I figured it was time to talk to Charlie, and also to Cal, about the seriousness of our relationship.

One night, William escorted me to a quaint Italian restaurant for dinner. I knew it must be a special occasion—William wasn't always so comfortable in public places. We spent the evening laughing, telling stories from our youth, and making plans for the future. At the end of the night, William and I walked under the night sky, the stars illuminating our path.

"I love you, Amelia. No matter what happens, I want you to know how much I care about you and Charlie."

We paused in the middle of the street. The light turned red, but I didn't care. I pulled him into my arms and kissed him, wanting him to feel the love I carried for him.

I looked deeply into his eyes and uttered the only three words I could muster that could even begin to encapsulate my feelings for him. "I love you," I said.

Despite our troubled pasts, we found a way to start fresh with each other. We maneuvered this cruel world, finding solace in one another. I loved him madly, and I knew he felt the same. Who knew the unlikely pair who fumbled for things to talk about as they sipped coffee on a bench so many nights ago would fall deeply in love? I never expected to, and yet here we were, kissing under the moon in the middle of the road.

Not surprisingly, the talk with Charlie went far smoother than when I spoke with Cal. My ex-husband worried I was rushing into something and it would not be beneficial for Charlie to have William around so often. I wanted to remind him he married the woman he cheated on me with and left his family for, but I held my tongue.

"Cal, this is my decision. I've talked to Charlie about it, and he's fine with me and William being together. I am not asking for your permission, but extending the courtesy of keeping you in the loop."

William overheard me speaking with Cal and promptly took the phone despite my protests.

Of course, that shut Cal up right away. I mean, what man in his right mind would challenge an Army vet? Not many.

Even though everything seemed to be falling into place, I could sense something still bothered William. Throughout therapy and having Bart around, I noticed drastic differences in his demeanor, including sharing a lot more and talking about past wounds. However, I sensed he still held something back.

"Babe?" I asked one night after I switched the TV off.

"Yeah?"

"Everything okay?"

"Of course. Why?"

"I just feel like something's off, like there's something you're not telling me."

"Oh," he said flatly.

I held my breath, hoping I didn't scare him away. Even though his communication skills had increased tenfold, he was still a man, after all.

"There *is* something on my mind," he said.

"Tell me." I drew circles with my fingernail on his forearm, attempting to soothe him into submission.

"I do like my job at the law firm, but I think there's another path for me."

"Are you going to quit?" I asked nervously.

"No, no. But, there's something else I want to do, too."

"What's that?"

"I want to create a place for guys like me," he whispered. "When I was on the streets, lost and lonely, I had nowhere to go. Sure, I had the homeless shelter, but...I had no one to talk to. Nothing to do. I wanted to better myself, but I didn't have the tools or resources."

"Mhmm. That makes sense. What are you thinking?"

"I want to open a place for vets or the homeless, or anyone who needs help, a place they'd feel safe going to. There could be games like darts or pool, a place to hang out or talk to people. I think it would help others and give me the purpose I've always felt I needed."

"That's an amazing idea, babe. I think you should do it!"

"You think so?"

"Absolutely. We should start looking for space as soon as possible."

"We?" William asked curiously.

"I'd like to help, too, if that's all right with you?"

"You'd help me?"

"I'd help you move a mountain if I could."

"All right. Let's do it," William said with inspiration oozing from his voice.

"I wanna make it right, Amelia. I need to do some good in this world. I want to make my dad proud. Hell, I want to make my mom, Spence and Hudson proud, too. I owe it to them to do something important."

"I understand, babe. And, don't worry—after we're done, they're going to make you a goddamn saint."

Chapter Thirty-Six

AMELIA

I learned a lot about William in the next month. I learned he's motivated as hell once he sets his mind to something and that he cares about the people he loves. He showed me just how big his heart is, and with the help of a few other attorneys at my firm, we secured a lease for the center. Ross chipped in several thousand dollars toward the lease. Despite my protests, he said he wanted to help. Plus, it would look good for the firm. William proudly named it "Survivors' Space."

One wall of the space, located a few blocks away from our office above a yoga studio, donned chalkboard paint for visitors to sign in, draw a picture or leave their mark. Another wall was lined with a clothesline with a Polaroid camera on a table to the side. William wanted visitors to feel comfortable sharing their experiences, making new friends, and documenting their journeys. He envisioned the clothesline to be full of full of photographs of smiling men and women who visited Survivors' Space.

At the back of the space stood a refrigerator, a sink, dishwasher, and a long wooden table which sat at least fifteen to twenty people. William and Charlie came up with the idea of having a Sunday dinner every week where people who needed a hot meal or a place to go could come and make themselves at home. While we didn't have space or a permit to house people, we wanted those in need to feel comfortable joining us during the day before we closed for the night. We did team up with the homeless shelter, though. Men, women and children could come here for dinner or to enjoy our space, then head to the shelter for a good night's sleep. We even hired a few retired veterans to drive guests from our space to the shelter at night.

I'd never seen William so happy and focused. When he told me he needed a purpose in life, I didn't understand just how crucial it'd been for him to find his path. But now that he'd found it, every cell of his body radiated hope and happiness. I thanked him every day for allowing me to be a part of his journey and establish this space for others.

We opened on the first day of Spring, a Sunday, which was very fitting considering it was a fresh season and a fresh start for both of us. Press, friends, and families lined up for the ribbon-cutting outside of the retro brick building. The sun shone, and birds pleasantly twittered about. William wore a grin across his face. Nerves rattled him, but they didn't show.

William in a new plaid button-up with dark jeans and myself in a pink floral dress stood before a flashing camera. Charlie, between us, held the oversized scissors as we prepared to officially open the Survivors' Space to the public. Karen was there and handed out flyers and buttons to those in attendance, too. Even Uncle Jimmy came to the ceremony. Bart was also a part of the celebration as he lay down in front of us all, lounging on the sidewalk and soaking up the sun in his bright orange jacket.

Joy filled me to my core as I thought about all the people we'd help in the coming days, weeks, months and hopefully years. I wondered how many Williams were out there, alone and lost. I wanted to help them all. I wanted to mend the broken pieces of their lives. It was selfish, really. It made *me* feel damn good to see others happy. Maybe I was doing it for myself, but I think in the end it didn't matter, as long as the people I helped had a chance at a better life.

The crowd chanted and counted down from three to one, and Charlie, William, and I cut the ribbon together. Karen, who stood behind us, tossed rainbow confetti into the air; Ross clapped and congratulated William and me, and Charlie whooped and howled with glee. We'd brought the community together and awareness to those in need.

William waved his arms, trying to gain the attention of the reporters and bystanders alike.

"Thank you! Thank you, everyone, for being here today. You know, my father once told me money couldn't buy happiness, and I'm here today to prove to him that he's wrong. Money *can* buy happiness as long as you're purchasing the right kinds of things. Money paid for this lease. Money paid for the furniture. Money paid for the food inside the fridge. And money will pay for future additions to come.

"If you don't already know, my name is William Divola, and less than a year ago, I lived on the streets. I was homeless and hopeless until this woman found me and wormed her way into my life." William paused to kiss my check and allowed time for the crowd to applaud.

"Amelia taught me about pushing forward and stopping at nothing to accomplish my dreams. If it wasn't for her, I might still be on the streets or even dead.

"Today is a new day, though, and a fresh start. Survivors' Space is a place I know I will call home, and I hope others will feel the same."

The crowd applauded politely, their eyes glued to William.

"In honor of new beginnings, there's something else I need to do," William said, his hand shaking.

Before I knew what hit me, William gazed deeply into my eyes and bent down on one knee. The crowd gasped, and my heart stopped in my chest. Was this happening? I wanted to scream for someone to pinch me!

"Amelia Montgomery, you are the light of my life and my soul-mate. I want nothing more than to call you my wife as well. Will you marry me?"

Adrenaline coursed through my veins. I never expected to see a man down on one knee before me again. And yet, there was William, stealing my heart away for the zillionth time with a modest, yet gorgeous diamond in his hands and an eager sparkle in his eye.

I turned to Charlie. "What do you think, bud?"

"Mom, William and I already discussed this." He rolled his eyes. "I gave him my permission weeks ago!"

I smiled broadly and turned back to William. "Yes!"

Everyone erupted in cheers, cameras flashed, and William slid the ring onto my finger: a perfect fit. He picked me up and spun me around. At that moment, the rest of the world blurred around me, and all I saw was this amazing man and the love he carried for my son and me. While I never thought I'd get a second chance at love, William had proven me wrong. I couldn't wait to start the next chapter of my life, to begin again with William and Charlie by my side.

EPILOGUE

When I look back on my life, some of the first things that come to mind are sorrow and heartbreak. I lost my father when I needed him most. I lost my mother when she needed me the most. I lost Spence and Hudson when our brothers needed me the most. So much loss and death—it was enough to shatter anyone.

Living on the streets, I grew thankful for the little things, like waking up with sunshine kissing my face and being able to find scraps of food every few days. But, through it all, I never gave up hope. I knew somehow, someway I'd find a way to stay alive and start again. I wasn't sure when or where my fresh beginning would come until I met Amelia.

This woman opened my eyes to a whole new world. She accepted me and helped me when no one else would give me a chance. She opened her heart to me with no strings attached. She loved me unconditionally and helped me start over, helping me begin again.

Snowflakes floated down from the cold, gray sky and landed on our heads. We sat on the bench I used to call home. Amelia rubbed her belly and squealed with delight.

"He's kicking!" she cried.

Charlie and I carefully put our ears against Amelia's belly, and the warmth of happiness melted the winter around us. My son would arrive in a few short weeks, and our little family would grow by one.

I was terrified of what was to come, but I knew with Amelia by my side, we could accomplish anything we set our minds to. Charlie couldn't be more ecstatic to be a big brother again. His half-sister carried a special place in his heart, but he secretly told me he always wanted a little brother. I told him I always wanted a son, and now I had two.

Even when life kicks us until we're down, it always finds a way to pick us back up again. Two years ago, I slept on this very bench with nothing but a tattered coat and my dog tags. Now, I had a beautiful wife and a family. While my material possessions significantly grew in quantity since my days of homelessness, there was one valuable lesson I learned that trumped everything: it's never too late to start over, and it's never too early to begin again.

The End.

ACKNOWLEDGMENTS

Let me start by saying that writing in a new genre was incredibly terrifying, yet exciting. This book wouldn't have turned out the way it has without my incredible beta readers. Mary, Sylvie, Chelsea and Sal, I couldn't have done this without you!!! Thank you for your guidance, suggestions and support.

Krista, thank you for your continued support and for being my editor. I'm so happy to have met you!

Lindsay, Gino, Nathan, and Jordan, thank you all for your service and for providing insight to help me build William's story. Couldn't have done it without you!

Thank you, Julie for creating my beautiful cover and always helping me with my never-ending design questions. Grateful to have you in my life!

Thank you, Mike for supporting my passions and dreams! I love you so much.

Last, but certainly not least, thank you to all of my dedicated readers!!! I wouldn't be where I am today without you and all of your support.

ABOUT THE AUTHOR

Laurèn Lee was born and raised in Buffalo, NY. She loves hockey, chicken wings and craft beer. She enjoys spending time with her friends, family and boyfriend.

Reading and writing are her life's passions. As a child, Laurèn became enamored with the Harry Potter series. As an adult, she loves psychological thrillers and mysteries with a twist.

We'll Begin Again is Laurèn's fifth book.

Make sure to sign up for her email newsletter to be the first to know about new releases, sales and giveaways!

https:www.laurenleeauthor.com/subscribe

ALSO BY LAURÈN LEE